For De
Wonderful Mother

WOMEN RISING

John Sant'Ambrogio

ISBN 978-1-957077-01-7

This book available at online bookstores.

Publishing assistance by BookCrafters, Parker, Colorado.
www.bookcrafters.net

Dedicated to my children

Stephanie
Sara
Michael

My grandchildren

Bella
Brie
Sebastian

In memory of my mother

Isabelle Sant'Ambrogio

CHAPTER

1

AN OMINOUS VISITOR

It was Saturday night, the evening Annie and Steve Carter and Jane and Bob Porter usually reserved for their get-togethers. The Carters, who lived in a beautiful mansion up on the hill, and the Porters, who abided in their small house below them, had developed a great friendship in spite of the fact the families often had different points of view.

The doorbell rang and Steve rushed to the front door to greet Jane and Bob.

"It's so great to see ya both," Jane said. "What did you bring for dessert? Is that pecan pie and ice cream? Wonderful!"

Jane brought the food into the kitchen and asked Annie if she could help.

A few minutes later, Annie stepped around the corner into the dining room, where Steve was starting to set the table. "Looks like you've got the table ready, honey," she said. "We're almost done in here, too."

Bob, sitting twenty feet away on the living room couch, laughed. "Hey Steve, that's the women's job."

Steve chuckled as well. "No, Bob, I'm taking it over 'cause she's paying me a hundred dollars per setting." They both laughed, and Bob returned to watching football on TV.

Suddenly, the kitchen, dining room and living room filled with strange vibrations, a slight shaking sensation. An eerie light shone through the window. Steve rushed out to the front porch, with Annie, Jane and Bob following closely behind. They all looked up at the sky. A meteor like sphere orbited above them, much bigger than any star, planet or even the moon, their eyes and mouths opened wide, an audible gasp coming from Jane.

After a few minutes it was gone. "What on earth was that?" Annie asked.

Nobody had a quick answer. "Wow, that was crazy. What are we supposed to do with this? I wonder if our neighbors saw it..." Bob said.

They slowly walked back into the house, looking at the sky every few steps. The night sky shone normally--all evidence of the meteor-like orb gone. When Steve stepped inside, he noticed the buzzing, slightly shaking vibration was no longer in the house.

"Either it was just us crazy folk seeing things, or everyone around here saw it. Jane, you need to find out," Bob yelled.

Jane started to respond, but Annie grabbed her wrist. "I wouldn't... not the way he talks to you."

The women carried steaming plates to the dining room and placed them on the table. "Kids!" Annie yelled. "Time to eat!"

After talking a bit more about the unusual incident, the two families seemed to forget about it and engaged with the kids in typical dinner table banter. They caught up on the latest news happening in town.

Three weeks later, Steve stood next to Annie to begin preparing supper and noticed she seemed taller. She was as beautiful as ever, beginning with her fetching green eyes, but she was also taller than him. She wasn't wearing high heels, and her normally casual clothes fit snug and tight.

Steve shook his head, all possible explanations for her sudden height explosion falling by the wayside. "I can't be shrinking, can I?" He also noticed she was eating much more than usual.

After dinner, they relaxed in the spacious living room of their open concept floor plan home, and watched the CBS Evening News. An unusually large number of scientists were being interviewed.

"What are they buzzing so excitedly about?" Annie asked as she sat down with two steaming cups of herbal tea.

Steve patted the sofa next to him, motioning her to sit. "That object we saw in the sky the other night." His eyes shifted back to the TV.

Scientists continued to discuss and analyze the strange meteor-like sphere that had recently circled the globe and shocked everyone, and how it was affecting humans. "To be more precise, women," one scientist added. The prominent Harvard expert thus echoed the opinion of the others interviewed. He felt the sphere's vibrations affected feminine DNA all over the country and perhaps the world. Women's appetites were increasing, and their bodies were growing taller and stronger.

Steve and Annie looked at each other. "Annie, can you stand up next to me for a second? Let's go in front of a mirror."

When she did, they both were shocked. There was no doubt Annie had grown recently. And quickly at that, the kind of growth spurt they'd last seen with their daughters or Jane and Bob's sons. They measured her at 5'9", an increase of four inches in three weeks from the height she'd been since the day she turned 15.

Steve hugged Annie because he could see she was in tears and very frightened. "My clothes don't fit anymore," she cried, reaching for a tissue. "Oh dear, oh dear, I knew something was happening to me, but I just tried to ignore it."

Which is precisely what most women were doing, but obviously, everyone knew. The CBS News piece confirmed that. Now that the truth was out, further ignoring of the situation, thinking everything would be the same, amounted to ignorance. Instead, confused citizens of all walks seemed to be asking, "When will this effect cease, and how harmful is it going to be?"

It took another three months for doctors and scientists to come to the conclusion that there were no harmful effects from the vibrations. However, the growth in women had not ceased. In fact, it continued increasing measurably. Whenever people stepped on the streets, they found women were becoming stronger and taller than most men — including many of their husbands. It sent the nation and world into social and cultural turmoil, and a constant topic on the news. When would this unbelievable growth syndrome end? What could it possibly have to do with a random appearance of a strange object in the sky, one that only hovered for a few moments?

Six months after the strange vibrations entered the earth's atmosphere, the uncontrolled growth of women's bodies stopped. Most women were now two and even three feet taller than they were before the sphere's effect. Girls in school were teased and called giants or Amazons. The women's clothing industry skyrocketed in sales, though high heels had fallen out of fashion in favor of flats. The demand for bigger, flatter women's shoes was matched only by a sudden need for men's boots with taller heels. Grocery stores struggled to meet the new food demand. It was a different world.

CHAPTER

2

CRAZY CHAOS

The six months after the sphere's visit were perhaps the most turbulent in the history of mankind. No one knew what to think. While the abnormal growth of women finally ceased, most in the world had not started to contemplate what this change in the human species would mean for civilization. Was everyone too stunned to think about it? And how would society change? People were blown away by the changes happening to the ladies, fearful another growth spurt would come, and it was never going to stop. Early studies confirmed that virtually all women on the planet had grown two feet or more. However, all the ramifications of the phenomenon had yet to be considered.

One evening during supper, Steve sensed a palpable sadness on Annie's face, her eyes dull, her gaze downcast, her normal broad, joyful smile flipped upside down into a perpetual frown.

"Annie, I love you. Even though you're two feet taller

than me, and we spent so much money on new clothes for you, I still love you," he said teasingly. "Your size has nothing to do with my love for you. I love you for who you are. Your new body hasn't changed all those wonderful feminine qualities of warmth and tenderness you show me and everybody else.

"And yes, your gorgeous blonde hair still knocks me dead. It hasn't changed a bit. Maybe a little longer and more proportionate, but never so beautiful as now," he joked. "And I just love your incredible long eye lashes."

"Steve, I don't know how I can survive this without you. You are a true man." She stepped up and began to wrap her arms around him. "Now for a gratitude hug..."

"Sure, just don't squeeze me too hard; you almost broke a rib last night," Steve said. "Remember, I'm kinda short and skinny now."

Annie kissed him on the top of his head. He continued feeding her only the love and joy she could feel, her unhappiness over what was happening hit her deeply.

Her morose attitude about the dramatic change in appearance didn't seem to be the case with Jane, who was thrilled with her new size. Although the Carters and Porters both believed families should consider themselves teams, Bob Porter felt he was the quarterback. He certainly looked like one, with his broad shoulders and muscular arms. He was tall and handsome in spite of his graying hair, and strong, too. He loved Jane deeply, but he felt it was his job, and his God-given right, to order her and the two girls around. Not only that, but in his view, the man of the house made all the important decisions for the "family" without any need for input or feedback from Jane or the kids. On the other hand, Steve never ordered anyone around, outside of occasional admonishments to their teen-aged boys. Annie was his equal in decision-making, his partner in life, the other half of what she felt was a strong mixed doubles team. Theirs was a partnership of equality.

With her new long dark hair and bright smile, Jane loved the fact she had grown so much taller and stronger, now even stronger than Bob, a brute of a man who could carry seemingly everything. This physical change to all women reinforced the sense of empowerment. Enrollments in women's movements had skyrocketed the past few months.

She walked into the kitchen, where Bob was stirring the stew, one of the few oven dishes he cooked. In his view, one that had kept families and their taste buds happy for generations, women cooked in the kitchen and men barbecued.

"Wait Bob, I'll move the breakfast table so we can dine more comfortably," Jane said. "Just keep stirring the stew."

"Jane, please stop ordering me around," Bob snapped. "You make me feel like a little kid."

Jane flashed a playful grin. "Well, you are little in size compared to me," she replied.

A bewildered Bob answered with a troubled look, "None of this makes sense! It's not right. What happened to the caveman theory, the Biblical scripture that women are to be submissive to their husbands? Huh?

Does that just get tossed out the window because you're taller? Not in the Porter family!"

Jane laughed. "The cave woman theory has taken over, I guess." She paused, then as a second thought she added, "Bob, since I'm now stronger than you, perhaps you can learn how to cook, get the kids properly dressed in the morning, drive them to school, clean the house... And, I could take over your job shipping and handling supplies at the plant."

"Jane, how can you talk like this? Are you kidding? They would never hire you. And I'd never let you out of the house for a hard, demanding job like that anyway."

"You wouldn't, huh? Really? Last week I secretly had an interview with them about a job, and they were really excited about my application. They liked that I'm almost seven feet tall, and still growing, with super strength that now allows me to load far more material faster than men – even you! They were so excited that they offered me a higher salary than yours, but I thought I should be fair and talk with you first." She peered intently to his eyes, watching doubt and irritation cloud them. "Hey, did you hear that? Me talk with you first before making a 'family' decision. When was the last time we did that?"

Bob simmered for a moment, then cleared his throat. "What's going on here? What am I supposed to do now?" he softly muttered, "Since I'm the quarterback, I should decide what to do next."

"Bob, you always said we were a team, and you were the quarterback. Now that I'm so much bigger and stronger than you, I am tempted to make myself the quarterback, but no, we instead are going to become a mixed doubles team."

"A mixed doubles team…"

"Like Steve and Annie. They make decisions together, run their family together, with equal authority and each has a say. Look at how loving and happy they are. It works. So let's work this out together."

Bob remained silent for a moment. "Jane, if our income is going to increase because of you, then I guess you should work at the plant. Maybe we can then buy a bigger house like the Carters on their hill that overlooks these Northern California meadows I love… reminds me of home. But I don't want to do all those things you've been doing around the house."

"Oh yeah? Who is going to do them?"

A fierce, angry look replaced Bob's sense of confusion. His face reddened. Jane could see it was probably best if she stopped lecturing him. She sensed he was very troubled. "Don't worry Bob, we'll get some paid help, and we can both work."

But Bob did not perk up. He was not happy they were both going to have the same job, and Jane was going to be paid more for her work than he was. His deepening unhappiness seemed the exact opposite of the rising sense of joy, happiness and strength Jane continued to embrace.

Up the hill at the Carter home, Annie felt really down. The only thing keeping her going was her husband's comforting love he continually expressed. Each morning Steve hugged Annie and told her, "You look so beautiful;

you are so majestic, so beautiful. Your height doesn't take anything away from your glorious being but watch your head by the fan. Maybe we should use a floor fan to keep us cool."

Annie wiped tears from her eyes and gently returned Steve's hug. "That talk show last night on CBS really brought to light the traumas we are facing in this country; in fact, in the entire world. On the one hand, I guess some of the women, though certainly not all, in Saudi Arabia are quite happy about the situation. Most Saudi women liked things just the way they were before the sphere's visit — or those whose husbands allowed them to be interviewed said they did — and are so unhappy with the turn of events. But now others have told their husbands they were going to drive, whether the men liked it or not. Those guys reportedly feel so intimidated by the size of the women that they give them the car keys.

"I guess things aren't all bad. But Steve, I hate it. I can't stand it."

"Honey, I understand. I don't know if this will make you feel any better but look what's happening in the inner cities. Remember what we heard last week on the news? That psychologist, Raymond Bates, claimed fewer husbands were running away because women's superior strength enabled them to prevent their partners from leaving. They often searched them out after they tried to desert them, grabbing, pulling them back to their apartments and telling them, 'You ain't going anywhere! You're gonna take care of the kids 'cause I got a job'."

Annie's lips widened into a slight grin. "I've heard and read studies that show wife abuse is disappearing, and rape doesn't seem to exist or be an issue anymore. I know sexual abuse in colleges has all but ceased, and sex trafficking has dropped.

"But Steve, honey, I know all these facts, and they certainly are helping some women — but not me. I loved it when you were able to pick me up and twirl me aro—"

"Honey we can still do that," he interrupted.

Steve strode over, picked Annie up and started to twirl her around. Unfortunately he didn't realize how long Annie's beautiful legs and feet were, and she knocked over the precious old flower pot on the coffee table, breaking the pot. Annie's new weight caused Steve to fall down, and she practically crushed him when they landed on the floor.

"See what I mean? With this terrible new body I'm so afraid, when I cuddle with you in bed, I might crush you when I put my arm on top of you."

"Annie, I know. I understand, but just because you can't put your arm on top of me doesn't mean we can't sleep next to each other and be close."

Annie sighed, and Steve whispered, "Dear One, it's not your size or strength or even your beauty that defines you. Love defines you. You express love now as you always did. I saw you help our older neighbor the other day. You ran out and helped him unload wood from his truck. That was so kind of you."

"I had to...he used to do things like that for me."

Steve butted in. "And your size hasn't stopped you from being a great editor for the local paper."

They heard a knock on their door. "Steve, I think our wonderful neighbors are here."

Steve rushed to the door and gave Bob and Jane hugs. He warned Jane to watch her head as she reached the door jamb. She ducked and followed Bob into the living room. "Well, I brought the delicious salad with pineapple again."

"Thanks, Jane. The chicken is almost done on the barbecue."

"Great, I'll go out with Annie to help finish the cooking."

Bob slumped on the sofa with a downcast face. "How are you putting up with this mess? Women taller than men think they call the shots now and can push us around and all...

"Oh, I guess it's a mixed blessing. I'm bearing it. How about you, Bob?"

"I'm not bearing it. Not at all. This ain't the world I want to live in."

Steve felt sorry for Bob and paused. He knew he needed to say something upbeat, to change Bob's mood. "Well, as we have all been hearing on the news and talk shows, I guess some problems in the world seem to be resolved, and it's helping the women's movements too."

"Yeah, that's what a lot of people are saying. Not that I don't care about others, but this is a disaster for me, and I don't know how I can deal with it. I was born a man. Men have always been the leaders. Look what's happened at the ballet, those who have been able to re-do their shows for this new thing — now women are tossing the men around! I sometimes feel like Jane wants to toss me around, and she's trying to be the leader in our family. I don't care if she is seven feet tall, she can't be the leader. I can't stand her attempts at role reversal. Men have been in control for thousands of years and women have been in their rightful place the whole time — under our leadership and control. Worked the whole time...why not now?"

Steve squirmed on the couch, uncomfortable. He and Bob had never had such a discussion. Steve didn't want to start an argument and spoil the evening, especially because Annie had been counting on the get-together with the Porters to raise her spirits. However, Steve's lawyerly skills were forcing him to step forward.

"Bob, before this crazy thing happened, weren't women starting to be treated more equally, at least in our country? Maybe this sphere is teaching us something."

"What?" Bob asked. "It ain't teaching me anything but the need to hold onto our traditional roles a little tighter."

Jane and Annie burst from the kitchen, smiles on both of their faces. "Supper is ready."

Steve was grateful for the interruption. Despite being a successful lawyer, he didn't like testy arguing. Unlike some lawyers, he just wasn't the arguing or cynical type, and operated with a lot of humility and compassion for his clients and the world at large.

CHAPTER

3

THE RUNAWAY

After a delicious supper, the Porters and Carters and their teens – Steve and Annie's two boys and Bob and Jane's two girls – gathered in the living room to watch the CBS Evening News. The President was addressing the nation to talk about all the challenges the U.S. and world faced during such difficult times. Many factions began fighting each other over traditional roles and religious practices, prompting the President to try to calm the nation.

"My fellow Americans, these are trying times for us, and I urge us all to have patience with each other. No one could have foreseen this situation, so I urge everyone to be patient and have compassion for each other."

Jane and Steve agreed with his statement, but for different reasons. Jane was thrilled to the point of elation with the turn of events. She enjoyed the fact that she could finally take over the quarterback position if needed, though what she really craved was perfect equality in all decision-making, family rearing, and life choices with Bob. It wouldn't happen overnight, though.

I hope everybody takes time to make decisions, she thought. *I don't want to see us rush into this. Time will let everyone finally come to the obvious conclusion – women are just as productive and successful as bosses. With a lot more compassion to boot. If we push too fast, the men will fight us like crazy as they always do. We need patience, as the President is suggesting.*

The President finished his speech, "Many are still in shock at what has happened, so as I said, we must be compassionate with each other and be patient. The Bible tells us, 'All things work together for good, for those who love God.' We can handle this challenge by working together."

Steve agreed, but he did not agree with what he thought Jane was thinking, "now women are superior." He hadn't asked her; he just surmised his slightly errant perception. He felt, as he always had, that size and strength did not determine who we were or who should be in control. He believed no one should think they were superior. Steve had always been supportive of women.

Once the President finished his speech, the kids wanted to watch the NFL Game of the Week, and it was a good one: Cardinals vs. Packers. Sports had always been one of the more popular events on TV, drawing strong men audiences as well as the sports-loving women, but now they were the most watched programs in the nation besides news breaks on the sphere visit. Why? Because professional teams in all sports were stealing women from the women's soccer, baseball, even football and basketball teams. One example was Rachel Good, a 6'4" superstar forward in the WNBA who suddenly sprouted to more than eight feet tall after the sphere arrived. One of the NBA's most storied franchises, the L.A. Lakers, moved mountains and budgets to quickly snap her up. After she caught up to the speed of the men's game, she became a dominant center and a hero to millions of other girls and women. As well as the more evolved men. Because of her size, she didn't have to jump to dunk the ball. The fans loved the changes, but women's team owners were furious. All kinds of lawsuits were filed, the judges and lawyers wringing their hands and dealing with massive headaches caused by litigation over antitrust and contract law they'd never had to address before. This game was just beginning.

Further, some women's teams were trying to arrange games with men's teams before they lost too many players. It was turmoil, but the fans loved it. As for football? Women turned up as linemen – or women – and receivers, tight ends and quarterbacks who could see over every man on the field, wearing huge chest guards to protect them. That still didn't stop the few defensive backs among the women players from reaching over the heads of their opponents and intercepting passes.

Two impressionable and skilled young athletes sat in the living room, riveted by the game. Seventeen-year-old Susie Porter and fifteen-year-old Sara squealed with delight as the two families watched the game, but alongside them, eighteen-year-old Paul Carter and his sixteen-year-old brother Peter were not as excited or happy about what they saw. Even though Susie kept squeezing Peter's hand, her flirting confidence had risen from her growth post-sphere.

"Look at those arms on Dorothy Pence. She must really work out!" Susie shouted.

Peter and Paul were quiet. Despite their close friendship, cultivated over the decade since the Porters moved in down the hill, the kids were great friends, but the boys felt intimidated. The new, somewhat tense atmosphere permeated high school classrooms and athletic complexes across the country. Boys and girls felt more separate and confined to their corners than at any time since Title IX broke down gender barriers in school activities in the mid-1970s.

Finally, the game ended in overtime. "Okay kids, it's after 11. Time for bed," Jane announced. "Last I checked, you all have school tomorrow, and I'm not interested in seeing tired eyes and hearing excuses." She turned to Annie. "She isn't either, boys."

With that, the girls walked back down the hill, while the boys reluctantly said good night and sauntered slowly upstairs. The Carters and Porters sat in the living room, prompting Bob to quietly offer his gratitude for their company. "Thank you for who you are. In spite of this travesty and the fact we may see things differently, we are still friends. But I'll be honest, this whole mess makes me want to stop living."

The Carters and Jane were aghast. No one said a

word, but their faces showed their shock. Bob abruptly stood and walked out the door, without pecking Jane on the cheek, without so much as a nod to Steve and Annie. His walk was fast and nervous, his eyes focused on the other side of the door.

He didn't go home. He walked through the neighborhood, hoping to lose his deeply depressed feelings as he viewed the lovely clear night beneath beautiful stars and a gorgeous full moon.

Stunned, Jane, Annie and Steve quietly looked at each other.

Annie was the first to speak. "I share his feelings, but for different reasons. This has been a shock to both of us. None of us knows who we really are anymore."

"Well, I have to say, I don't much mind being someone different," Jane commented. "For years I have been the servant, the second in command. Bob never pushed me around physically or anything, but because he towered above me and would hover over me when he ordered me to do things, I often felt intimidated. Not anymore. Maybe his tune has changed. It's more like he's asking as he looks up to me, though I feel it's more out of necessity than sincerity. He still tries to talk down to me, though not as much. It's kinda fun to talk down to him now... physically, I mean."

"Well, apparently many women are delighted with what's happened," Annie jumped in, "but I'm not one of them. I don't like it at all." Tears formed and spread through her eyes as she left and scurried upstairs.

"Oh Annie, I'm so sorry."

"It's not you," she said, then walked into her bedroom and closed the door.

Embarrassed and concerned for Annie as well as Bob, Jane walked home.

The next morning, Jane returned before Annie left for the local newspaper. When Annie opened the door, she found Jane rubbing tears out of her reddened eyes, dark circles beneath them, mascara smudged. Clearly she hadn't slept all night.

"Bob never came home last night," she said, fighting back more tears. He hasn't called, and he doesn't answer his cell phone. He always answers when I call, if nothing else to tell me the next thing to do."

"Well, honey, maybe he needs a day to think about things," Annie said, wrapping her arm around Jane, pulling her into her shoulder, comforting her.

"I called the plant, and they say he never showed up for his early shift," Jane continued. Annie's soothing words floating over the fear piercing her heart. "The plant is really pushing me to work for them. I'm gonna have to sign up if Bob stays away; we don't have much of a cushion to fall back on." She paused for a moment, sobbing. "At least I'm grateful Susie is old enough to drive. But oh, I am so worried about Bob... so worried this is all proving too much for him, and he... and he... I'm worried he ended his life."

Annie pulled Jane into her chest. "Jane, don't go there. Please. He's only been gone maybe fifteen hours. I'm sure he's not the first man who just needed to get away to try to make sense of all this. I sure understand, much as I hate what has happened to, well..." She looked herself up and down, almost feeling vertiginous over her harrowing new height.

"When is the last time you tried him on his cell?"

"Right before I walked up here," Jane replied.

"And?"

"Goes right to voice mail. Like I said, he always answers. And never shuts his phone off."

"Okay, give it the day. If he's not home, call the police and we will get a neighborhood search going. Maybe he just slept on a friend's couch who understands how hard this is on him."

"I've already called the police. They won't do anything till he's been gone 48 hours, but they said once that time comes, they will get busy."

"That's good."

Jane rubbed her face on Annie's shoulder, instantly moistening it. "Lord, forgive me," she said, eyes buried in Annie's shirt. "I've been too hard on him since the table turned on us physically."

Annie hugged Jane and tried to comfort her. "Jane, this is not your fault. This is the sphere's fault. In some ways it's society's fault. If we had been more compassionate and patient with each other, as the President begged us to be, maybe we wouldn't be going through all this."

Steve came down the stairs and took in the sad scene in the foyer. "What's going on? Did Bob settle down last night? What's wrong?" The ladies were still holding each other, and Steve sensed what happened. "Oh, my goodness. So, Bob never came home last night? I'll call the office and tell them I have an emergency."

This was not an ideal time for personal emergencies. His office was loaded with a multitude of cases. There were all kinds of legal disputes caused by the sphere's visit, disputes for which there was no written or previously settled law, requiring hours of additional eye-burning research and strategic thinking to even form an argument for his clients. However, Steve always put friends first, and this was a no-brainer. He had to help his neighbor before anything else.

"Jane, I'll start driving through the north end of town. You and Annie deal with the south end," he said, launching into solution mode.

After driving for hours all over town, checking in again with the police and sending out emails to all their friends, there was no trace of Bob.

A day later, Annie posted a notice in the paper about Bob's disappearance. After a week, there was still no sign of him and no word from the police, who as promised launched an investigation and spot search at the 48-hour mark. Annie and Steve did all they could to comfort Jane, Susie and Sara, with Peter and Paul also helping out, their lifelong training as compassionate teens being put to work in a tough situation. Seeing Susie and Sara cry eased their feelings of intimidation.

As more time passed, their fears grew, especially considering Bob's angry, depressed frame of mind when he walked out the door after dinner. Had he ended his life? Disappeared without a trace? Started a new life somewhere else?

The questions only increased their anxiety and Jane's feeling that the worst had happened.

CHAPTER
4

A CHANGED MAN

Six weeks passed without a peep from Bob or a positive update from the police, who now were dealing with several additional cases of missing men. Even additionally assigned detectives and search squads barely covered the growing list. Jane fought back tears, frustrated by the latest call to the station, as she walked slowly to the mailbox, hope and dread filling her in equal measure.

Moments later, the mailwoman pulled up and stopped, not at the mailbox, but just past it. She handed Jane a few pieces of mail, then held the final piece. A letter. "I think you want to see this, Jane," she said, handing over the letter.

Jane looked down, saw the familiar scratchy but legible writing. Bob!

After quickly reading the letter, her tears increased as a smile formed on her face, like a rainbow cutting through a torrential mountain downpour the second a hint of clear sky and sun appeared. She ran to the Carters to share it with them, her body suddenly feeling light, relief beginning to flush out six weeks of pure dread. Steve and Annie sat on the sofa while Jane read Bob's letter out loud to them.

Jane, forgive me for leaving you and not letting you know where I was. I was so depressed that I was tempted to end my life, and then I met some men who were in the same boat as I was. As I put my sadness aside for a moment, I began to find some joy helping others to cope with the problem of feeling inferior like I did.

As I met more and more men challenged the same way as I was, who left their homes because they too couldn't cope with women's new height and how we can't be... like we were... I came up with an idea to form a group devoted to helping men deal with all of it. I'm calling it MM.

Annie quipped, "He must mean AA. M&Ms sound like candy."

"No, it has a name. Merciful Men," Jane said. She went on:

I have formed MM to help men like me, so shocked by this change in our lives, that we have come close to mental breakdowns. The meetings help us deal with the fact that we no longer are the 'big guys in town.' I think most of us have had to give up our chauvinistic tendencies. I know I did. If this crazy thing hadn't happened, I'm not sure if I ever would have changed. So Jane, I hope you will forgive me. If you want, I will come back home, because I think I'm getting better at dealing with this disaster.

As they listened to the last word, there was a knock on the front door. Steve went over and opened it. "Bob! That you underneath all the hair?"

Bob stood still, a nervous smile on his face. He looked like a man who'd spent six weeks wandering or sequestering like a hermit, his hair longer and curly, his beard thick and unkempt.

Jane ran to the door, staring at him for a moment, seeing the fear and contrition in his eyes. She walked up to him, and they wrapped their arms around each other. When the Carters moved in for a welcoming hug, Jane swung her arm wide and took in all of them, their faces came together in the middle like the close of a prayer circle. Or a football huddle.

Steve realized how important this moment was for the Porters, and they needed to spend time alone with each other said, "What a blessing this is from the Lord. Let's all say good night and let our dear friend return to home, where he'll be so welcomed."

Later that night, Steve shouted from the bathroom, "I'd love to know what this group Bob started does to help men as troubled as he was. How do you think they deal with the present crazy world?"

"Beats me. I'd like to know, too," answered Annie. "Maybe I can start my own WW self-help group. Let's see, maybe 'Worried Women' or 'Wonderful Women'."

"Or 'Wimpy Women'," Steve chuckled.

"No," Annie countered. "Pretty sure I can prove to you we're not wimpy. Wishy Washy Women' is better."

They both laughed as Steve turned out the light. The joking lifted Annie's spirits, and before they fell asleep she added, "Or maybe Bob would let me join his group and help men and women work together to deal with this mess."

The next morning, TV news reported that terrorist organizations all over the world were awash in turmoil because women were rebelling. Apparently they were joining together in groups, grabbing men's weapons and refusing to abide by the commands of the caliphate leaders.

"Wow, this change certainly has affected the Middle East," Steve said as he flipped a stack of pancakes expertly from griddle to Annie's plate, followed by his own.

"I know," Annie said. "There's no question that this has brought some good to the world, but it certainly didn't to me. At least I don't see it. I know I shouldn't complain, but I want to be who I was, not who I am. Look at me." She shook her head. "A walking freak show."

"You and several billion others, apparently," Steve said. He put down the spatula, took her hands and peered upward into her eyes. "Remember what I keep telling you. Your physical size has not changed the way I see you, and the love and devotion that always flows from your heart to me and everyone else. And it never will."

At breakfast the next day, Jane asked Bob, "So tell

me, since you apparently spent six weeks figuring this out silently away from us, without so much as a note to let us know you were all right... what is the message of the MMs?"

"As I see it, there isn't just one message. There are many, but one thing that united us was that we all need to understand who we really are," he replied, his voice unusually calm and level, not the commanding boom that instantly took over any room or conversation. "We have to learn that we're not just big or small, not just good looking or a little less than good looking, not just young or uh ...maybe mature. No, we need to grasp the fact that we're more than big or small, red or green, in a physical body.

"When I was away, we found that when we recognized ourselves spiritually rather than materially, we saw a different path to follow."

"Who, honey? Who is 'we'?"

"Men like me who left their homes because they couldn't handle our diminished role with y'all growing like you did."

Jane nodded with understanding, her eyes fixed on Bob's. He didn't waver, and his eyes shone with a luster she couldn't recall seeing before.

"We felt so intimidated by y'all's new size that our sense of self-esteem fell through the floor—"

"You mean your sense of control? In your particular way?"

Bob nodded in agreement. "Fair enough. When we realized we couldn't grow in size, just like we couldn't after turning eighteen or whatever, we began to see that we could grow in another way, in character. We decided to remember that before all this happened, women asked to be treated equally. So, we men don't have to feel guilty for asking the same thing, right?" Bob laughed at his own sarcasm.

"Oh, my goodness, Bob, you're blowing me away. Who took over your body and mind? What made you come up with all of this? It doesn't sound like you at all."

Bob began, "Honey, it..."

But Jane interrupted him, "Bob, what's going on here? I call you 'honey' all the time, you never reciprocate ... but you just said it without my hopeful prompting."

"I guess one of the things we're learning is to be more affectionate to our wives, even though they can push us around now."

Jane leaned across the table and clasped his face with her hands. "Bob Porter, or whoever invaded my husband's body, it is so good to have you home as this new person. Although, honestly, very few of the women I know think of this height change as a ticket to pushing their men around. Only the ones with real axes to grind, or who are tired of years of being mistreated. No matter how hard you've been on me at times, I am not in their camp. I just want my husband home."

"Truth is, I'm calling you 'honey' because I love you. Even if you do push me around, I'll still call you 'honey,'" he laughed. "I used to push you around and you still called me 'honey.' Anyway, the real reason is when I look across the table and see you, I feel the same sweetness in my heart now."

Jane kissed his cheek and pulled her hands away. Who was this guy? She couldn't take it all in. She didn't know whether or not to believe him. Was this the real Bob?

Annie woke up early, troubled, and started thinking about Bob. How did he handle his depression? She thought she was the only one depressed, but now she knew that wasn't true. The previous night's special MSNBC broadcast moved through her mind like a jigsaw puzzle finding its own pieces, a full hour devoted to the challenges facing so many women. *Many of us apparently don't want to be superior — or inferior,* she thought. *Maybe we should start a WW group, like 'Wise Women,' or maybe 'Wonderful Women' or 'Women Winning.' No, that would just scare the men.*

Steve interrupted Annie's thoughts as he rolled out of bed. "Good morning, dear. You're up early."

"I've been thinking about Bob, and this crazy but wonderful change that seems to have come over him."

"Me too. It's wonderful that he's back safe and sound. Would you help me carry that heavy old sofa out to the street so the junk truck can pick it up this morning?"

Annie nudged him. "Take a look out the window, Steve."

"Oh my gosh, it's out there already. Who'd you get to help you?"

"No one. I moved it myself last night. I knew they come early to pick up and I didn't want it taking up space in the garage for another week."

Steve was stunned. "Annie, how…"

"Well, as I said, things aren't all bad," Annie chuckled. "I know that the few times I come out of my gloom seem to be when I have the most strength to help others. And it's fun when I get something done that a man couldn't do before. I've decided to talk with Bob today to see if he'd let some women in his club."

"Go for it," Steve yelled over his shoulder as he headed for the office.

Three months later, the MM group had evolved into a far bigger organization, Men & Women Together, now included both men and women in Merrydale. The support organization already listed over 50,000 members throughout the country, its mission to help men and women deal with the shocking changes and providing a badly needed outlet. The Porters and Carters, worked together, and originated, organized and were now leading MWT. Women's groups were very supportive. Bob Porter was its president, while Annie jumped in as vice-president to reflect the group's commitment to serve women and men equally.

Annie and Bob became local celebrities, and once the national media got wind of what they were doing, national and international personalities. In short order, the President met them at the White House to praise what they'd done.

In addition, frequent appearances and interviews on TV news and talk shows gave them opportunities to publicize their vision and message: The important things in life were not measured in sheer physical strength and size, nor the ability to use that to manipulate or control others, but the amount of love, compassion, kindness, tenderness, and wisdom one expressed. Forget traditional standards of who was the biggest and strongest, ethnic background, gender or what your religion was.

The Pope, along with several seven- to eight-foot nuns, invited them for a rare private sitting in his quarters in the Vatican. The visit also included a special visit to a place Annie always cherished in pictures and stories, the Sistine Chapel, featuring Michelangelo's amazing ceiling mosaic with the fingers of God and man touching at the center point. Heaven touching earth. Rather than being subjected to the typical two-hour tour through treasures of antiquity the Romans and early Christians acquired through war and occupation, followed by a strict 20-minute-only peak at the Sistine Chapel roof, the Pope ordered a one-hour tour of chapel only for Annie. She looked up, tears of joy in her eyes, visibly moved at Michelangelo's vision and peerless skill, his ability to channel God into humankind through his brush... *the ability of all of us to find our God-fed purpose and change the world with it,* she thought.

Many of the world's religious leaders were getting on board with their message. All seemed to be going very, very well, Annie thought as she gave the Sistine Chapel and its immortal ceiling one final peek, this one for her soul and spirit.

CHAPTER

5

TWO POINTS OF VIEW

A multitude of men and women throughout the world agreed with Bob and Annie and MWT's mission, but many others were passionately opposed to their views. It boiled down to one thing: those who could see their way forward in a rapidly transforming world, and those who clung to the old traditions and roles of women and men.

Soon, another organization secretly formed and gestated in Merrydale and fanned around the country: the TGs, or Tough Guys. Their hatred for Bob and Annie and what they were doing motivated Soapy Strong, a corporate CEO and the city's most distinguished businessman, to gather many like-minded buddies together to talk about the mess they felt they were in, especially the men. They had no problem being labeled "chauvinistic" by society; they reveled in it. They rejected the idea of "let's live with it," or "if we are sweet and nice, they won't push us around." They stuck with "we men are still the bosses."

Some women were joining the TGs. They weren't comfortable being bosses, and they liked staying home and welcoming their bread-winner husbands when they returned after a day at work. After all, that work supported the family, and being taken care of was great. Who else but women could care for the home, anyway? Men? They liked focusing on being attentive mothers and loving housewives, regardless of their superior physical size and strength. Who needed the pressure of competing for jobs? This new idea of changing women's roles seemed terrible. "Just leave us alone," was their motto. "Besides, this size advantage could just be fleeting."

Soapy took in all that was happening around him. He knew many who would accept his approach to deal with the chaos. He had his secretary print flyers, which he distributed to friends and employees; the more receptive employees then spread them out to their friends in person and online, creating a viral sensation.

In just the first month, Soapy attracted over six hundred men and women to his weekly meetings in an abandoned church. Soon other TG groups started throughout the country. All members pledged to keep silent about plans and ideas discussed at the meetings, and all were required to sign strict confidentiality and non-disclosure agreements.

In spite of the rapid growth of TG, MWT continued to amass the greater public support. The TGs were not getting nearly as much news coverage, and invitations to appear on talk shows were few. They received some press, but it wasn't always helpful. One editorial labeled them unfairly as the new Ku Klux Klan, labeling things they didn't understand, which seemed to be an unfortunate social practice before the sphere arrived to throw all labels and roles out the window.

All of which led to the latest Tuesday TG general meeting, a discussion in a packed conference center to address the lack of opportunities to get their message out and the need for more publicity.

"Look, one of the reasons MWT is doing so well is Bob Porter's charisma," Stormy's most trusted lieutenant in the TG's, Jeff Monty, said. "In spite of the shock and confusion created by that horrible sphere, he is succeeding in reaching people. The truth is everyone is uncertain about what we should be doing. How do we face the new female giants and Amazons? Unfortunately for us, Bob Porter was the first to offer a solution. Even if it's not a good one – and I think it's a social disaster that plants the wrong ideas in women's heads – people think his approach is great.

"Soapy, you have more charisma than Bob. So let's get you out there on the air."

Immediately, six hundred men and women rose to their feet, yelling with enthusiasm, "That's what we want to fight for," one shouted out. "Give us the boost on the air, Soapy."

Three days later, Fox News agreed to bring Bob and Soapy together for a Sunday morning debate.

Jane questioned Bob's willingness to meet and debate Soapy as she deftly balanced four breakfast plates on her long arm and laid them neatly at the table. She turned to face the back bedroom. "Girls? Breakfast!"

"Bob, do you really think this is wise? Why should you even give him the opportunity to appear on TV with you?"

"Honey, he's already started to go on TV and other talk shows, and frankly I don't think the commentators are questioning him in ways that reveal the dark side of TG's philosophy, digging in their male superiority heels against a rising tide against it. That never ends well. TG's lies need to be countered. I'm hoping I can start the process to get the truth out. Our country, before the effect of the sphere's invasion, would have labeled his philosophy as 'crazy misogyny'. But the unbelievable disaster that has hit us has knocked us unconscious. We don't know what to think or how to think. You know the mental challenges Annie and I went through; millions of other men and women are experiencing the same feelings.

"It's urgent that we be there for everyone. We must help them get through this mess as Annie and I did. There are just so many undecided voters – just like before the last presidential election. Remember how the debates changed the outcome that November? We need to stop this crazy movement in its tracks and not let it get its roots in the soil."

"Maybe you are right, honey. We probably shouldn't let the TGs get overconfident because of their success," Jane finally agreed.

As the sun set and the clock struck seven the

following Saturday, there was a knock on Soapy's door. It was Jeff Monty.

"Oh, hi, Jeff," Soapy said, his greeting gruff but friendly. "What's up?"

"Soapy, someone has talked to me privately about wanting to do something drastic to stop MWT's growth. I promised to keep it a secret, but I feel I have to tell you."

"What do they want to do, Jeff?"

"Take down Bob Porter. Kill his movement once and for all."

Soapy stood for a moment in stunned silence. How did his peaceful vision to keep things status quo, trigger several in the TG's this way instead?

"Jeff, that is absurd," he said. "I never heard what you just said. Go tell your friend he should forget it."

The following morning, Bob and Soapy stood a few feet from each other backstage, getting a touch-up in the makeup room and going over their respective talking points for the televised 9 a.m. debate, just a few minutes away. Moderators Ralph Master and Mary Reed had put together a series of tough questions both Bob and Soapy would have to answer. Neither moderator, tough journalists in their own right, was about to let either man off the hook with a half-baked answer or a canned response that sounded like a cliché or blatant sound bite. Not on their show.

Mary was 7'5" and Ralph 5'11", prompting the stagehands to set up a chair for Mary fit for a third-grade classroom, and a stool for Ralph set to maximum height.

Except for sports, TV directors were doing everything possible to hide the huge disparities in the sizes of men and women. The station and network expected up to ten million people to watch the debate, and they didn't want to make any mistakes, beginning with the presentation of their hosts.

At 9 a.m. Bob and Soapy walked into the studio and sat on their chairs.

Ralph began the debate. "Good morning, Bob of Men & Women Together, and Soapy of Tough Guys. Thank you for joining us to help us make some sense of how best to move forward with our lives, our treatment of each other, how we grow our radically changed society in this new world. We are happy to have you here this morning as the nation and the world are facing these daunting challenges, some of the most complex in our history. We are hoping you will give us your ideas on how the human race can deal with these challenges."

Mary added, "You both lead fast growing organizations that help people cope with these challenges, though in totally different ways."

Ralph asked the first question. "Bob, why do you feel your groups have the right answers to deal with our dilemma?"

"Well, for one thing, I'm wondering if this dilemma is really teaching us some lessons," Bob said, speaking slowly and calmly, his level-headedness still causing Jane to shake her head as she watched side-stage. "For thousands of years, we have approached male and female relationships in a very biased way. It's been 'the bigger the better' rule. The strongest is supreme in everything so we thought, and women have had to struggle to be heard. Now that we face a situation where women are bigger and stronger than most men, we are forced to question the truth of that former societal practice. Many millions of men will trace it back to following Biblical scripture, and their narrow interpretation of it. Me included."

Tears formed in Jane's eyes as she realized, in Bob's answer, just what he'd been doing his six weeks away. Transforming into the beautiful man now on stage.

"Does this mean men must now be subservient to women?" Bob asked rhetorically. "That possibility has frightened and depressed many of us, men and women. But when we take the physical out of the picture and focus on the many other wonderful qualities we all possess – in equal measure I might add; it's a matter of how we access these qualities inside – well, the world changes. It has to. How do you fight off inner change carried into our daily lives, by millions? MWT feels that this is an opportunity for men and women to be equal, regardless of size and physical strength, something that has not been the case for centuries.

"I know we think the sphere brought about these unbelievable changes to women, but before all this happened, many women had already shifted into breadwinner roles, plus still caring for their still-taller husbands. Unfortunately, it didn't seem to have much effect on the way many men thought, and I was one of them. I routinely ordered my wife and daughters around; I put them down; I had to change."

Jane grabbed a tissue from a stagehand and wiped her eyes. "You okay, ma'am?" asked the stagehand, like Jane, a 7½ foot tall woman.

"My husband... I've waited twenty years for this man on stage to show up."

"So maybe this event needed to happen to wake us up," Bob continued, moving toward conclusion. "MWT is helping men and women deal with changes and return to peace and sanity, be filled with joy as they see the real kind man and the real tender woman. We try to not look at the physical bodies but rather look at wonderful spiritual qualities we all possess."

"Thank you, Bob," Mary spoke. "Soapy, how do you look at all this?"

Soapy couldn't wait to counter Bob's points. "If you study the Bible, you will find so much written about men being the leaders and given authority over women. Women are told to obey their husbands."

Annie and Steve watched the debate on TV in the Carters' living room, after Annie decided not to attend, to allow Bob to focus on his specific points and not feel the need to accede to hers. "Here goes Soapy, I just knew he'd bring the Bible in to try to state his case."

"For thousands of years, it's been the men who have led the people and the nations," Soapy explained, his voice powerful and authoritative, the voice of a highly successful CEO whose business fanned across many nations and fueled a good part of Merrydale's economy and job market. "Once you give women equal power or, heaven forbid, supreme power, the world will be in chaos. Look what Delilah did to Sampson. Look what black widow spiders do to their mates. They kill them. With all the physical power women have now, they could soon betray us just like Delilah did. We must pass laws that will protect men.

"I know this might sound crazy to some, but maybe there should be better gun control. Starting with these tall, suddenly empowered women. Perhaps women shouldn't be allowed to have guns. Or loosen up the laws now to allow open carry. Now that they are so big and strong, they could hurt us if we don't openly carry guns for protection. Men have had supreme authority up to now, and that brought much of this world to economic prosperity and a sense of balance in society."

Soapy paused to sip his water while Ralph, the moderator, furiously scribbled a question on his notepad. After putting the glass down, Soapy moved into his conclusion to opening remarks.

"To be a great leader, you must have the qualities of inner strength and courage. And most men have these qualities. Bob says to focus on the spiritual qualities. Well, men are the ones with the best spiritual qualities. Think of Moses and Jesus."

Ralph turned to Bob. "What do you think of what Soapy claims?"

"Well, if you were going to quote the Bible, I would suggest some other quotes. In Genesis, we learn that God created man, male and female, but I don't think God said one was supreme. It seems to me we are created equal, not one superior to the other. And in

Galatians 3 it says, 'There is neither male nor female, for ye are all one in Christ Jesus.' I think that reinforces what I feel we are. We are more than just a male or female body, much more than physical forms. You look inside, to our hearts and souls, and we all carry much the same qualities. It's how much we open those up to our families and the world that truly will change things, heal and bring more peace to this situation, to the world.

"We should also remember that women, not men, were the ones who stayed with Jesus while He was on the Cross. And again, it was women who discovered His empty tomb and announced His resurrection to the male disciples. There is no doubt that women played a very significant role in the Bible."

"Hooray!" Steve yelled on his living room couch.

"I second that," Annie said, her smile spreading ear-to-ear.

"I just feel that spiritual strength is possessed equally by both men and women. Actually, I feel we have to forget the physical body in order to grow spiritually," Bob concluded.

Mary turned to Soapy. "Any more thoughts, sir?"

"I'm afraid I'm not convinced by Bob's comments. A lot of men I know wouldn't buy into his arguments. I think the proof of who's right will be determined by the future size of our organizations, the ones that gather the most people. By the way, we have both men and women in the TGs. There are lots of women who don't want to be superior or equal. They enjoy having men be in charge. They enjoy the traditional lives they've lived in perfect happiness, raising their kids, cooking, being there for their men. Why make them change, too? They love to sit back and let the men be bold and brave, no matter how much we can make fools of ourselves, which I admit. My wife sure has some stories. It makes them feel safe."

Ralph chuckled. "All right, that's a worthy measure, Soapy. We will see which grows the fastest, TG or MWT. Next month we'll check your attendance."

After the debate ended, Bob and Jane rushed over to the Carters. When he walked in the front door, everybody cheered. They all hugged him, including all four kids, who emerged from the upstairs rooms.

"You were great, Bob!" Steve shouted.

"I'm glad you agreed to do the show, honey," Jane added. "I was wrong. Don't listen to my advice for you and MWT anymore... unless I order you to take out the garbage." She chuckled as she drew a playful frown from Bob.

"Well, I'm so glad you thought I did well. Soapy is a tough smart guy. Now I just wanna relax and eat some barbecue chicken. Got any?" Bob asked.

Annie laughed. "Yup, we have some just for you."

The day ended on a high note, great food, love and friendship during the rare lunchtime barbecue, everyone buoyed by the belief MWT was winning the battle.

Unfortunately, the battle had just begun.

CHAPTER

6

THE PLOT THICKENS

Soapy was not happy. His seven-foot-tall, soft-spoken wife Mabel tried to console him, but with no luck. Soapy sat down to eat the delicious dinner she prepared for him.

"I can't stand that Bob. I sure hope the viewers didn't buy into his nonsensical diatribe," he said, grousing on almost every word. "He's not right about anything. But he has a lot of charisma and it's helping him to build MWT. We gotta stop him. Mabel, what did you think about the debate?"

"Oh, I thought you did just fine." Actually, she didn't sound too enthusiastic, her tone of voice was one Soapy knew over the years meant "not too great." Soapy got the message. After he finished eating, he gave Mabel a hug and kiss, thanked her for her support and went to bed to grouse some more.

The next day at the TG's board meeting, everyone was furious. "Bob Porter is crazy. We gotta get rid of him," many of the members shouted. Soapy didn't say anything for a long time, his expression long, forlorn, sad.

Finally, things quieted down.

"Ladies and gentlemen, I ask you to ponder our challenges. We need to get out there and talk and talk and talk. We must tell our members to hand out our flyers and network with as many people as possible. When they see a giant woman with her normal sized husband, ask them to hand him the flyer. If they look at all interested, take a few moments to chat with them."

Jeff Monty interrupted. "Soapy, all your ideas are great, but this requires something a lot more powerful and definitive than talk and flyers. We gotta take Bob down. By whatever means necessary, as I see it."

The rest of the TG board nodded in agreement. Soapy dropped his head and then put up his hands. "No, no, we can't do that. Just the thought goes well out of bounds from any solution that will grow our organization. That'll just make us a social pariah."

He quickly walked out of the room. Like it or not, Soapy knew that a terrible seed had been planted.

Another organization incensed with the circumstances was the Mafia. Jeff had a friend in high school who was a member. After the TG board meeting, Jeff took out his cell phone. "Tony," Jeff spoke quietly on his phone. "Could we get together for some pasta tonight?"

"Sure." The voice was gruff, accented, almost a growl.

But friendly. Jeff had not talked with Tony for months and was elated they might get together again.

After dinner in a small Italian restaurant, Jeff started the conversation. "Tony, are you finding it tough for you guys with all the women turning into these Amazonian bullies trying to control their husband's lives... or worse?"

"Jeff, it's hell. Many of the wives are bullying their husbands, just as you implied. So many are buying into that crap from Bob Porter. He's building such a huge gang of guys and dolls, all of them feeling empowered to change the way we like it, to change society, which of course will ruin our culture, our way of life, even the businesses we, um, oversee in this area. That meeting Bob and that Annie woman had with the Pope is cutting into our power. He's a showman. Many of our guys are so confused, and they don't know what to do next.

"But I'll figure it out, and when I do, you'll be the first to know."

Jeff nodded and smiled. "That's all I could ask for, Tony... but I think there already is an answer."

"Really?" Tony responded with a puzzled look.

"The bad guy here is Bob Porter, and he has to be eliminated...and you guys can do it. Once he's gone, the MWT will shrink."

"Yeah, much as we've gotten away from handling things in that way, I think you're right. This is a situation that, I agree with you, calls for it. Let me raise the idea with the bosses."

Two days later, Tony had an opportunity to speak

with Giovanni, the Mafia boss in Merrydale. "Giovanni, you think we could solve some of our problems if Bob Porter disappeared?"

"Yeah, we've been thinking about this for several weeks, more than thinking actually. I think we have put together a great plan. One of our gang made contact with a young American guy, name of Madido, who has become radicalized by watching a lot of online recruiting tapes pushed out by those crazy terrorists in the Middle East. He likes the idea of assassinating Bob for the glory of one particular radical terrorist group. And I guess his own glory, I don't know. Of course, the stupid kid doesn't know that our guy Mr. X, who's been talkin' to him, is in the Mafia. He thinks Mr. X is just a terrorist sympathizer—you know how we sneak into every group in town. Our plan is to put the blame on terrorists, and of course they'll blame the Muslims."

"Wow, Giovanni, that's a great plan! When are we going to pull it off?"

"I can't tell ya, but it'll happen soon. And, you may be a boss, Tony, but I'll tell you what I'd tell anyone else. Keep your mouth shut or the plan goes away—" Giovanni snapped his fingers — "just like that."

Tony left, promising to keep quiet and assuring Giovanni he had nothing to worry about.

CHAPTER

7

BETTER WATCH OUT, BETTER NOT CRY

The MWT was growing by leaps and bounds. Bob was becoming as popular as an A-list movie star or Hall of Fame athlete, and Annie, as vice-president, was gaining great notoriety. She also was becoming the symbol of how to use recent events not only to empower herself, but spread that strength and confidence to women otherwise confused or uncertain about their places in a post-sphere world.

On December 12th, Bob and Annie were scheduled to arrive at the Town Hall for a rally and presentation. The auditorium had a capacity of over a thousand people and was expected to be sold out. Certainly, the evening would carry the fervor of a partisan political rally, but there were no politics at play here. Only the desire for men and women to continue joining forces for the sake of national and global society and security.

"The Town Hall meeting is the perfect setting for

Madido to assassinate Bob," Giovanni told the bosses. "Get to Mr. X and tell him to buy Madido a ticket. Give him a pistol with a long barrel for accuracy. Mr. X should take him to the Town Hall early to check things out. And be sure the gun has no history so it can't be traced. Be sure Madido practices so he doesn't miss. Madido is willing to be caught and die for whatever radicals have been plugging into his brain online, and he believes he'll go to heaven and have seventy virgins awaiting him for this particular service to Allah. He thinks the terrorists will be proud of him."

While playing their weekly Scrabble game with the Carters, Jane said to Annie, "It's wonderful that you and Bob are going to be speaking together at the Town Hall rally. It shows how men and women can work together."

"That's true, Jane, we do work great together at MWT, but hey, be careful not to peek over at my Scrabble letters! Just 'cause you're tall and can see everything, that doesn't give you the right to cheat."

"I wonder who has W R T S U M and an E." They all laughed.

"I'm told that more than a thousand people are coming to the rally," Steve said as he added up his score. He was the winner, but no one cared. They just loved getting together and never really competing, unlike their kids, who were playing mixed doubles ping-pong in the basement. The fierce grunts, cheers and shouts of intense athletic competition filtered upward.

"Okay, you four superstars, it's time for bed," Jane

said. "My two, head on down the hill. I'll be there in a few minutes."

The kids rushed up the stairs, excited about the game they were playing. And sad because Susie and Sara were on their way home. Because the girls were so big, playing mixed doubles was a challenge, and they had to be careful not to hog the show. It was hard for Peter and Paul to squeeze in because Susie and Sara's long arms crowded them out. But they came up with a new rule that made it more fun for all of them. You had to stay on your side of the table, and if you reached over the middle, you lost the point. It made it more fun, and the boys didn't seem so intimidated. Plus, Susie and Peter made it a point to exchange a few pecks on the cheek, their teen romance blossoming and reminding them ping-pong is only a sport, not a fight to the next breath.

Everyone shouted cheerfully as the Porters left for home. "See ya tomorrow at the Town Hall. Girls, watch your heads on the doors," Steve said.

Madido arrived early at the rally to scope out close-in shooting angles. He didn't know which side of the stage Bob would occupy, nor Annie's place, so he settled on a prime seat, center row front, not thirty feet from the stage. That way, it wouldn't matter who stood where. He was dressed in a dark suit, dark tie and white shirt, his stout .357 Magnum pistol tucked in an inside coat pocket, the silencer alongside it. He needed to twist it onto the barrel before the full audience filed in. He also had a camera strapped around his neck.

50

Madido didn't want to attract attention to himself, so he sat down and quietly pulled out a book, pretending to read it. He didn't want to talk to anyone or otherwise be distracted. As he held the book close to his chest, he removed the silencer and affixed it to his .357. He held the grip, checked the chamber – six shots would be plenty – and clicked on the safety.

As he finished, the audience began streaming into the auditorium. Two seven-foot women sat on either side of him, probably early twenties, he thought, just a couple years older than him. He regarded their innocent faces, their sense of awe as they chattered about THE Bob Porter and THE Annie Carter, as if his targets were Gods themselves. Madido snickered. There was but one Allah, and these two pretenders were not it. He might be only nineteen, but he'd already figured out the world and what it should be under Sharia or at least some traditional law — and Bob and Annie needed to be eliminated to make the path for his handlers a lot easier. He'd also heard something about Tough Guys mentioned in passing, but really, who could be tougher or more righteous than he after he made himself immortal with two clean shots?

One of the girls cleared her throat, staring down at him from her height. To Madido, she looked like she was leaning in from the sky boxes at a ball game. "Sir, would you move over one seat so we can sit next to each other?" she asked.

"No, with all due respect, I'm sorry I can't move because I'm taking pictures of the rally for the Merrydale paper. This is exactly the right spot for me to catch them as they speak, wouldn't you agree?"

"For sure," the inquiring girl, Betty, replied.

"You'll get direct shots on them from here… great photos," her accomplice Barbara added, taking her seat.

How right she was, without knowing it, Madido thought. "I won't be staying for all the speakers, since my, um, editor just wants the two MWG leaders, so one of you can take my seat when I leave…"

Or get killed by the police, who would arrive and think of the girls as the shooters, he thought.

"Okay, we get it, but don't stay long," they chuckled softly.

When Annie and Bob walked on the stage, a tumultuous roar greeted them. They bowed, smiling, and sat down. Bob's chair was so tall it was a struggle for him to get up on it. Madido started to contemplate the best time to shoot Bob. If he let Bob speak too long, he mused, it would allow him to spread more fake news crap, to use the universal buzzword for discourse one might personally disagree with. But to his surprise, Annie and Bob walked to the edge of the stage and began to sing "Oh, What a Beautiful Morning."

Madido was elated. Perfect. They were standing on the lip of the stage, a few arm lengths away. I'll shoot Bob when the applause is loudest and he bends over to bow, taking his eyes off the audience. Madido put his hand in his jacket, held onto the gun, and planted his finger on the trigger. As they sang the last words of the song, Madido pulled out the .357 cannon and took careful aim at Bob. The terrorists are going to call me a martyr. So is the entire world that believes in the one true God, Allah, all other spiritual and religious paths being pure blasphemy.

He waited for Bob and Annie to bow. He didn't wait long.

Bob and Annie finished singing and took their bows as the crowd predictably went wild. Betty and Barbara leapt off their seats and threw up their arms, applauding their heroes as if they were rock stars at Madison Square Garden or the protagonists of a sensational opera in Verona. As they whipped their huge arms into the air like a pair of human windmills, Barbara knocked the gun out of Madido's hand before he could get off a shot.

It fell on the floor. The young women looked at each other in shock when they saw what Barbara had knocked out of Madido's hand. Then they looked at Madido, who was still pointing his hand at the stage.

"Why did you bring that?" Betty asked, her soft voice of minutes ago shaking and hard.

Madido looked at her, his eyes black and fierce as the end of time. "Why do you think, infidel?"

"I don't think so!" Barbara yelled. She and Betty reached down, grabbed the much shorter Madido by his arms and dragged him across the aisle, their superhuman strength and size easily subduing his desperate, thrashing attempts to break free. No one else seemed to notice anything beyond, say, two girls helping a suddenly sick or feint friend, because the crowd was so raucous, their cheers visibly moving Annie and Bob, who continued bowing and smiling with no clue that they'd almost been assassinated.

When the girls got to the lobby, they pulled Madido to the front doors. Rather than wait for police to come and arrest the would-be assassin, and shoved him out the door, hard. He landed on his belly, knocking the wind out of him. As he struggled for breath, filled with the humiliation of being manhandled by girls after his failed attempt, they closed the doors, ran back to their seats and grabbed the gun that nobody had noticed.

Barbara put the gun on her seat, and she sat on it. The audience finally calmed down, and Annie and Bob gave their great speeches.

When the rally was over, and the stars left the stage, Betty and Barbara shouted for one of the ushers. When he reached them, they pointed at the gun and told him some idiot tried to shoot Bob, even using the word infidel when they asked why he was bringing a loaded .357 Magnum into the rally. "Then we knocked the gun out of his hand, accidentally," Barbara said.

"So, where is this would-be assassin?" The usher looked around. "I see no one at the scene of the act except the two of you... and you're in possession of the gun."

"Well... well..." Betty stammered.

"Why didn't you report what was happening to us or a policeman? What did you do with the alleged shooter? Like help him escape?"

"No, we grabbed him and threw him out the door, face first."

"Well, that sounds like aiding and abetting an escape." The usher radioed for police units. "You care to elaborate?"

The girls knew they were in trouble. Betty answered, "One way or another, we decided he had to get outta here. He had to be removed. We didn't want to interrupt the show for everyone else or start a mass panic, so we like grabbed him and, like Barbara said, threw him out."

"Like the morning trash..." the usher said, a sarcastic smile creeping along his face, his eyes filled with doubt and suspicion.

"Which is what he probably is," Betty said.

"And," Barbara added, "since he was gone and the gun was on the floor, it seemed all right to wait until the rally was over."

The usher asked the first police officer to arrive, also a seven-foot woman, to talk with Barbara and Betty. They looked at each other, fighting back tears of pure terror. This wasn't going to be pretty. They disarmed the man, and for simply not running him into the arms of the first cop they could find, they were now in trouble. Big trouble.

"Come with me, ladies. We need statements from you downtown."

"Can we like follow you in our car?" Barbara asked.

The policewoman shook her head. "No, I'd prefer you have a seat in the back of my squad. I won't cuff either of you if you walk with me outside."

"But this is like just a statement, right?" Betty asked, her eyes now filled with tears.

"Yes... sure. A statement."

When they arrived at the police station, the girls were separated and put in different rooms. It didn't take long for either to realize this was not a statement session, nor a friendly interview. This was an interrogation.

The detective on call began with Barbara. "Young lady, in the 90 minutes or so we've had you here, we've been busy getting witness statements. I've got them right here, in front of me." She dragged out a file, already loaded with a dozen sheets of paper. "So far, no one has reported that they saw a young man being dragged up the aisle by two young women in the middle of the rally. Are you denying that the gun was yours? We checked the fingerprints on the gun and found only yours. Was he wearing gloves?"

"Yes," Barbara said, a little too fast. She then prayed that God would guide her on just how to respond. She realized that all she could do was tell the truth and that Betty would do the same.

Barbara told her eyewitness version of everything that happened. The interrogator looked like she didn't believe her story and left the room. Betty told the truth as well, but the police didn't believe either of them. They were fingerprinted, booked on a 48-hour investigative hold as material witnesses – and possible suspects – and tossed into different cells.

Now they were really in trouble.

CHAPTER

8

MANIC MADIDO'S JOURNEY

Within a few days after the assassination attempt, Madido knew he was in trouble, too. *What did the terrorist supporter who gave me the gun think? I won't be a martyr. I'm a flop. I can't even go home. They'll find me and kill me, and I won't be a martyr. No seventy-two virgins for me!*

As he passed a news stand, he spotted the banner headline in the paper:

TWO MERRYDALE WOMEN ACCUSED OF ASSASSINATION ATTEMPTS ON BOB PORTER AND ANNIE CARTER

He was shocked. This is not fair. They'll get all the credit from the terrorists. What will they get – 72 men?

Back at the Porters, the families watched the ongoing news coverage of the assassination attempt, disturbed by what they saw. Two young women were being held for an attempt to murder Annie and Bob. When they flashed Barbara's and Betty's pictures, Steve shook his head.

"Something's wrong here. Those girls look like models who haven't done a thing worse than steal mascara. Or ditch college a couple of times."

"I agree," Annie said. "This feels like a rush to judgment."

During the commercial, Jane said, "Bob, you can't do this anymore. You were almost killed by those two crazy women. You gotta quit!"

Steve piped in. "Bob and Annie, we've got to think deeply about this whole thing. I know you would hate to stop leading the wonderful movement you've created, but it looks like things are getting very dangerous. And, for my money, these girls aren't the assailants. This feels like a frame job, or as you said, Annie, a rush to judgment."

After some silence, Bob spoke. "I can't stop fighting for equality for us all."

Annie quickly added, "Nor can I. And... I saw something at the rally that I didn't think much about till now."

"What?" Steve asked.

"Those same young women now in jail dragging a little guy from front row center. I just thought it was three people who didn't like our singing, or a boy that got sick. I didn't pay much attention to what they were doing. Now?"

"Wow, we have to call the police immediately," Bob said. "No way it was them. I saw them too when we first came out. They were like cheerleaders, not dead-eye shooters."

Annie went to the police station to report that what she had seen from the stage was exactly what Barbara and Betty claimed had happened in one interrogation after another, the police working double-time to try to trip up the girls on their stories. To no avail. The detective in charge felt plenty of truth coming from Annie's eyes and mouth, took the girls out of lockup, and submitted them to lie detector tests in separate rooms.

They passed. Their stories were as consistent as the day they were held as material witnesses.

Then the police found a single thumbprint on the handle of the gun, smaller than Barbara's and Betty's, decidedly masculine. The real assailant. Barbara and Betty were assured they would be released soon.

After a hastily called squad briefing, a dozen cops fanned out to search for the would-be assassin who had been thrown out of the Town Hall by the girls. The Merrydale paper changed its accusatory tone promptly, under Annie's guidance as associate editor, now publishing reports that both praised and condemned the young ladies for the way they handled the situation. Bob and Annie began praising the girls during press interviews, leaving their poor judgment in freeing the assailant behind, happy to still be alive.

In a subsequent TV interview, Bob made several points to back Barbara and Betty. "These two women saved Annie's life and mine," he said unequivocally. "They knew if they started screaming, they might never have been heard over the noise of the crowd, and if they were heard, there could have been a stampede that would injure or even kill people. Many people. It was packed in there. They managed to subdue and drag the real perpetrator out of there, and no one was hurt. It is my understanding they have since given the police a good description of the would-be killer. I am confident he will soon be found, and his reasons for trying to kill us known.

Annie also stood up for the girls. "See, women having superior strength has paid off in this case."

One reporter asked, "Why on earth didn't they just strangle him if they were so strong?"

Annie rolled her eyes as Bob answered calmly. "Because no one in MWT, or who supports us, believes in killing to solve anything. We're just not that way."

Madido was living on the street, totally confused as to what to do next. Maybe if I get credit for trying to kill Bob, the radical terrorists will take credit for my attempt, and I can die a martyr. I don't want to live anymore anyway. The depression and sense of uselessness to society that had led him into the online clutches of the terrorists roared back in waves. I need to end it.

He walked into a library and wrote an anonymous note, stating that a man who matched his description in the newspapers slept on a certain street. He printed it out and dropped it off at the police station. He ran out before anyone could grab him.

That night, Madido was found by a squad patrol, picked up and imprisoned. The next day in a lineup, Barbara and Betty positively identified him as the man they had thrown out of the Town Hall. Madido promptly confessed to the crime.

Before Madido's confession was reported and it was thought Betty and Barbara were guilty, Soapy smiled in delight because there was new fuel for his campaign. "See, don't give guns to women," he repeated, his position gaining steam, at least in his own eyes. "Look what they do with them. We men need more guns." Even the NRA had jumped on the bandwagon to deny women the right to bear firearms, a flagrant violation of the Second Amendment. But they were women, Soapy thought. Who would really care?

But now that the truth about what really happened was out, Soapy bagged his idea and sought a new approach to attract attention. He joined the loud voices of critics furious that these big women had let the potential murderer go. "See, women don't know what to do. No man would ever have let the shooter go. Men are smarter," he said, his voice rising with an enthusiasm he felt about ways to sharply curtail or stop MWT.

Bob and Annie desperately wanted to support Barbara and Betty during this turmoil. They were so grateful for what the girls had done for them. The afternoon the ladies were to be released, Annie suggested, "Let's invite Betty and Barbara for dinner tonight and have them join our 'family'. It's the least we can do for them. They saved our lives!"

The Porters and Carters drove to the police station at twelve noon, when the ladies were scheduled to be released just a few hours shy of the 48-hour hold limit. As the girls came out with their families, Bob walked up to them. "Ladies, we are so excited that you have been set free, and we would love to have you join us for dinner tonight."

"Oh, that is so kind of you," Barbara answered, "but we will be joyfully spending the evening with our parents."

"Bring them too," Steve said. "We have plenty of room for you all."

That evening, the Porters and the Carters threw a celebration party of sorts for twelve guests. No one celebrated more or felt more relieved than Barbara and Betty, who just hours before had been staring at an attempted murder charge. Peter, Paul, Susie and Sara decided to add some spice to the evening, so they broke out their guitars, flutes and a violin, and traded off songs, solos, and duets kids played after supper. Everyone was elated.

CHAPTER
9

BUSTING BOB

Madido was in jail, and after the initial excitement over the arrest, things began to settle down. Everything seemed to be working out perfectly.

Sort of. Unfortunately, there was still trouble in the wind. Soapy was furious that Madido had been captured and that two girls were sharing the credit for saving Bob and Annie's lives. This compounded his initial anger over the use of violence in the first place. *Good thing the kid didn't get a shot off,* he thought, *although cutting the head off the MWT snake would solve all of my and the world's problems.*

Instead, MWT was growing even bigger, Bob and Annie were now elevated to even higher popularity and status as survivors of a botched hit. The country was slowly being persuaded that size and strength were not as important as character and wisdom. MWT was even using the Bible! As Bob had previously done on the first TV debate, they quoted Genesis. "In the beginning God created man and woman, but I don't see where He said one was better than the other," Bob claimed at MWT's rallies. "And if we are going to quote the Bible, maybe there's no difference between men and women. In Galatians, Paul writes, 'in Christ we are neither male nor female.'"

But that did not persuade Soapy. "They are not equal to us," he shouted at his latest rally.

The fervent partisan crowd screamed, nearly frothing as they basked in his philosophy to put women back in their places, keep men the head of households and businesses, politics, and law enforcement... basically every meaningful role in society. "Yeah! Yeah! Yeah!" They yelled as he fed them with one piece of traditional red meat after another.

But as supportive as the crowds were, Soapy noticed something else: they were getting smaller.

"We have to find some way to smear Bob," Soapy said later at a TG board meeting. "He's too perfect and his charisma is winning people over. Where are we going to be if things continue this way? We have to stop him."

Soapy's manager, Rusty, made a suggestion, "Maybe if we can find something in his past to shame him, something worse than the rumor that he controlled his wife – which of course would hurt our message – people will stop joining him."

"Great idea," Soapy said, "but that might not be possible. Our researchers have determined he's pretty much without skeletons in the closet. Maybe we could tempt him with one of our beautiful long-legged women members, photograph him with her and get it into the papers."

From that moment on, the board began to concoct a scheme to bring Bob down. They were able to get a gorgeous member, Abigail Sony, to join them. Along with the rest of the TG crew, Abigail disagreed with Bob's ideas, but she thought he was cute and charming. She imagined how great it would be to hug him, even caress him, anything to make him look like his wife was not the first woman he thought about.

"We need to spy on him," Rusty said. "Learn his schedule and find a time and place when he is alone, and then we can jump in and set something up. If we do it cleverly, he won't even know what we're up to."

They stayed up all night building a plan that all agreed was brilliant. Now to execute it.

After days of spying and following Bob, the TGs located an isolated place he visited routinely every day. Each evening, Bob picked up his mail at the post office and there was rarely anyone else there. The plan was simple. Just before Bob arrived at his usual time around 8 p.m., Abigail arrived and put the plan into motion. She and the others knew Bob was a compassionate guy and would immediately try to care for her if she needed help. That would be the beginning of the show, and it would be Bob's end.

When Bob arrived, he found Abigail lying on the floor beneath his P.O. Box, clad in a sheer blouse and short skirt. She looked like the end was near. Her eyes were closed, and she moaned softly. Bob rushed over and bent down to help her, and Abigail whispered, "Sir, could you lift me up?" Because she was whispering so softly, Bob had to get close to her lips to hear what she was saying. "Could you put your arms under my shoulders and lift me up off the floor?"

As Bob leaned close to put his arms behind her huge shoulders, Abigail grabbed and held him tightly and then kissed him. She was so strong, her arms and legs so much longer, that Bob couldn't pull himself away. Rusty and two other TGs rushed in and took photos of their embrace.

"What's this all about?" Bob shouted.

Abigail jumped up laughing. When Bob pushed himself up, she hugged him and rushed out of the room with the three men.

"Wait, wait. I wanna talk to you guys! Why did you do that?"

Then Bob realized what occurred, an obvious frame-up meant to humiliate and publicly embarrass him, and quickly left the post office and drove home.

He ran inside, still shaking, angrier than at any time since Jane started growing weeks after the sphere appeared. "Jane, you won't believe what just happened! I think I was set up by some of Soapy's men at the post office to make it look like I was having an affair with some huge woman."

Jane laughed. "Oh Bob, there is no way anyone in their right mind is going to believe you did anything wrong." With Jane's help Bob calmed down, and they shared a few chuckles before heading to bed.

The next day, pictures of Bob and Abigail appeared in papers nationwide. They were so convincing that even

Jane paused for a moment when she studied them. She wondered if it was really a set-up. The pictures showed a blanket under Abigail, and because they were enlarged and cropped, you couldn't tell where they were taken. But Jane quickly changed her mind and knew in her heart that it was a set-up to destroy Bob and MWT.

Soon, though, Abigail made the TV news and talk show rounds, claiming Bob was her long-time boyfriend. Bob immediate denied her claims, and the TG's propaganda at large. Still, the power of the media is such that many believe the first and loudest voice on any issue, regardless of its merits. Consequently, MWT faced the worst challenge in its short history.

At their weekly dinner at the Carters, Barbara and Betty, who were now a part of the "family," listened as Steve lamented about the mess Soapy created. "There is no question that this is a terrible scheme thought up by the TGs to discredit you, Bob."

"It has already cut our membership numbers," Bob said, "just as the attempt to kill us cut TG's numbers and rally sizes. I know we have to find a way to get the press to see the truth. But actually, what worries me the most is the guilt that Abigail must be feeling. She gave me one friendly hug before she left, and I feel that she was forced into doing this."

"Or," Annie said softly, "she knew what she'd done, and wanted you to know that she personally meant no ill feelings."

That night Bob pondered the situation before he went to sleep. Brilliant as he was, he could not arrive at a solution. However, one thing kept coming to mind. More than fearing what might happen to MWT, he felt more and more empathy toward Abigail, who, he increasingly believed, was forced into being part of this scheme.

CHAPTER

10

THE TRUTH COMES OUT

The next day, while being interviewed by CNN, Bob again denied that there was any credibility to the incident. He felt moved to reach out to Abigail. "Dear Abigail, I'm sure you must know what you are claiming is not true, but I forgive you. You were either forced into creating the incident or were convinced by some group to be part of the scheme. You are not the guilty party here, and I forgive you."

Abigail was watching the broadcast at her apartment and was so touched by Bob's comments she was blown away. She was alone and had some quiet time to contemplate the situation. She was pretty convinced of the TG's "man is the top" philosophy. She had a domineering father who ordered her around, but always provided for her. However, she was beginning to admire Bob as a person. She felt so guilty. She fell into a deep depression.

After a restless night with little sleep, Abigail

became convinced she had to tell the truth, no matter what philosophy she had bought into. She realized that once she spoke the truth, she was going to have to go into hiding. She went to the local TV station to find out how she might be able to make a true statement about what really did happen in the post office.

The staff went crazy when she came into the studio, and they quickly prepared to take videos of her when she recanted her story. The staff was so excited when they realized they would draw fantastic attention. They contacted their lawyers to witness the disclaimer.

Abigail testified that she had lied during a previous broadcast and that she had been persuaded to be part of a scheme. But she would not state who was behind the scheme, because she feared for her life. Once the video was complete, Abigail left the station. She drove home, cut her long hair, packed her suitcase and headed out of town. She knew she had to disappear from the world she had always known.

Abigail's disclaimer was on all the news stations, and the Carters and Porters breathed a big sigh of relief. Annie ran over to the Porters to hug Bob, who was so touched by the change of events he was in tears. That night everyone got together at the Carters and had a wonderful celebration. Barbara praised Bob and said, "Look what love and forgiveness did. Betty, maybe we should consider trying to love and forgive Madido."

Betty and Barbara looked at each other. Steve suggested, "Maybe if you visit Madido in prison and tell him we all forgive him, it will bring joy to us all."

Annie added with a smile, "Of course, women are much better at forgiveness than men."

Everyone laughed, and the evening ended with the kids playing a little Mozart and an arrangement of John Williams' "Star Wars" music.

CHAPTER

11

SISTERLY LOVE

Madido grew more and more depressed in his Perry State Prison cell. How did he become so miserable in his first 19 years that his happiness now depended on being recognized as a terrorist and committed to die? That only dying as a martyr would make him happy? He dropped his head to the concrete cell floor once again, tapped his slippered feet, and fought back more hard, bitter tears.

The days turned into weeks. His status as a prisoner in isolation, earned by trying to kill the immensely popular and influential man Bob Porter, prevented him from hearing any news on the case. He grew more and more morose. He began to realize that his happiness came from a different source, an outer source — knowing he was appreciated. This was a different message: now he never would receive that recognition.

Madido grew up in a loveless, broken family, one incapable of expressing compassion or empathy. The propaganda that he had been exposed to through the internet and phone calls from the Middle East affected him. The recruiter who called him seemed so warm, and he assured Madido that the radicals' cause was good and he would be rewarded in heaven with seventy-two virgins. So when Mr. X contacted him, he felt appreciated by the radicals. He didn't realize it was actually the Mafia pushing him to shoot Bob, and not the radicals. Now he was cut off from all that, alone in prison and never going to be rewarded in heaven. He probably wouldn't even get to heaven now. He would spend the next sixty years in prison, not emerging into society again until he was 80.

Then something happened that made him see a different heaven.

Barbara and Betty, along with Bob and Annie, implored the prison warden to allow the two young women to spend some time visiting Madido. The warden asked, "Why on earth should we allow them? That boy is pure danger."

"Perhaps we can find out who was behind the assassination attempt," Annie replied. "And these girls are confident they can build a rapport with him, since the three have already become acquainted, though not in a typical way."

A week later, the prison warden called Bob to tell him that, after much discussion, it was decided that Betty and Barbara could visit Madido. He suggested that they should take time to build a congenial relationship, just having a conversation, and not inquire too soon as to who was behind the whole plot.

"Understood," Bob said. It went exactly as Bob and the others wanted.

The next day, the prison guard entered Madido's cell and told him, "I don't know why you're so special, son, but two beautiful ladies are here to visit." He shook his head and began to grouse. "And we're going to allow the visit in the prison garden. Guard will be here in a minute to walk you out."

"I don't know any beautiful ladies," Madido said. "I don't want to see them."

"Well, they went to great effort to visit with you, son, so I suggest you consider that."

Madido thought for a second. *Whoever they are, I can at least spend five minutes with them.* "Well, warden, who are they?"

"The ladies that stopped you from shooting Bob Porter."

"Why would they see me? Last time I saw them was on my back after they threw me through the front door of the auditorium."

"Bob Porter personally vouched for them." The warden shook his head. "You ask me, they're crazy, too. But making the world a little more peaceful. Son, let's get ready."

Madido was shocked. He didn't know what or how to think.

When Betty and Barbara joined him in the garden, they towered over him. He kept his head low and didn't look up at them.

"Madido, we are here first to thank you for telling

the truth, which helped get us released," Barbara said. "That was very kind of you, and we appreciate it, and we appreciate you. That was very courageous. We and all our friends have you in our thoughts."

Madido couldn't believe what he was hearing. He had expected to be yelled at, chastised, criticized, and perhaps ridiculed, if the women were as mean as they were strong. Slowly he looked up at the beautiful giant ladies staring at him, compassion shimmering in their eyes. It may have been the first time in his life that he felt truly appreciated.

Numerous thoughts poured through his head, all involving a release. He knew he wasn't getting released from jail, but if he could get the burden of "sole suspect" off his chest, tell Barbara and Betty that he was just the trigger man, let them know who sent him...

Just the thought of following through lifted a weight off his chest, lightened his mood a bit. He sat opposite the women on a table in the stark rock garden, a guard fifteen feet away, peering at Madido in case the women tried to slip contraband or a note to him.

Then it happened. The love and compassion he felt from the women in the garden moved him to tell the truth. He had never felt anything like this before. "Ladies, the truth is—"

Barbara interrupted. "Madido, when you confessed to your attempt to assassinate Bob, you were being moved by something greater than all of us to tell the truth. Look what this has meant to the world."

Madido was in heaven. His whole consciousness

changed. His depression left him. "Maybe it was something greater than all of us that moved me."

Betty jumped in. "We've heard that you may have wanted to be given credit for trying to destroy someone who opposed the radical philosophy. At least that's what the reporters are saying, but you know, reporters…" She flipped her hand in the air, a half-dozen bangles jingling from her wrist and up a good eighteen inches on her arm. "But there is still something within you, greater than pride, that is now making you want to be truthful."

Madido was blown away. Here he was in prison for attempted murder, and his whole perspective on life was changed.

The girls were quiet. Seven-foot-tall Betty walked over to Madido and put her arms around him. "Madido, we care very much for you. You are so important to us. We'll be visiting you every week. Just let the guilt inside you blow away – like a mist."

Then the real shocker came as both ladies bent down and kissed Madido on each cheek. He couldn't believe what was happening. He'd never been touched or kissed so affectionately by a woman other than his mother, and she'd stopped being affectionate sometime before his fifth year of school.

The guard walked up, a fixed glare in his eyes. "Okay, Madido, you've gotten more love in ten minutes than most in here get in a year. Love fest is over. Ladies, visiting time is up. I need to escort Madido back, so if you wouldn't mind, time to go."

"We'll see you soon," Betty said with a broad smile.

A minute later, a joyful Madido smiled all the way to his cell and held that smile the rest of the day. Not that he had to try to hold it; the smile seemed to grow from somewhere inside him.

CHAPTER

12

FORGIVEN

It was a good thing that the Carters' living room was so spacious. The "family" was growing larger and larger. The Carters' mansion on the hill was far larger than all the other homes in the roaming neighborhood. People often asked why it was so much bigger than the regular floor planned family homes all around them. When the Carters bought the beautiful "castle" years ago, they thought they would love the four hundred acres of lovely meadows spread out below them. But they missed having neighbors and decided to sell the acres and start a wonderful and unique housing development. Other families could live right next door and become the neighbors they missed having.

Like the Porters.

The Carter home and its enormous living room was turning out to be an ideal place for the "family" to meet. The four teens were usually upstairs playing Monopoly or having a ping pong game in the basement. Or, in

Peter and Susie's case, carrying on their infatuation for each other. Bob and Jane, along with Steve, Annie, Betty and Barbara, would enjoy delicious barbecues or great potlucks, making the get-together evenings great fun.

"Oh, it was really a joy to meet with Madido," Barbara told the "family." "He looked like the most sullen, depressed guy we've ever seen when we got there, but by the time we left, he was smiling and actually returned our hugs. It was a magical experience for us."

Steve asked with a little smile, "Maybe we should call you both the 'FF's for 'Friendly Females'."

"You all, this is turning out to be something really special," Annie said. "We are working together and creating joy for each other. This, in spite of the fact that we have to deal with you little guys."

Everyone doubled over with laughter.

Betty swung her chair around, her long legs clearing the table. "You know, Madido went from being a little monster to a nice man in only a few minutes."

"Or maybe he was always a nice kid until he fell down that online rabbit hole with the terrorist group that influenced him," Jane said.

"More like infiltrated his mind," Steve added.

"I wish there was a way for him to start his life over," Betty continued. "It was obvious that a little affection made a great impact on him. I guess he didn't get much love in his life. Barbara and I will visit him again. Thank you, Bob, for inspiring us."

Annie piped in. "You know, loving each other is

probably what we should be doing more in our MWT meetings. I know so many of our women are deeply concerned about what has happened to them. And sharing their feelings has helped to ease the pain they feel. I know that being accepted by each other makes such a difference. And I know it broke the paralysis that depression caused me, which is why I joined MWT. Maybe we MWT women should focus more on finding ways we can help men who are suffering, too. When men finally understand that we can see them as they really are, not just as big or small, handsome or... well, maybe not so handsome, they are uplifted. We certainly want to make men feel loved and not use our superior strength to intimidate them like some men did to us."

"Sounds good to me," Steve said. "Annie, you know I always said you were beautiful in spite of the fact that your clothes were constantly busting on you every week, and you never said, 'Steve, just 'cause you're a skinny little guy I still love you'."

Another round of laughter rolled around the table.

Then Bob made another suggestion. "In keeping with our new approach to handling the effects of the sphere disaster, maybe we should try to find Abigail and invite her to be a part of our 'family' too."

Jane spread her arms wide. "First of all, that's a surprise coming from you, honey, even the new you. Besides, where are you going to find her? I think she disappeared after she came out with the truth. I know I would. She was probably afraid that whoever talked her into the scheme might hurt her."

"Well, Jeff Monty was behind the scheme. He was shooting the photos that framed me. And that boy would hurt anyone who didn't go along with him," Bob said.

"Well, any ideas?" Annie asked.

There was a knock on the front door. Steve opened it, and a tall lady with dark olive skin stood before him, wrapped in a shawl, possibly Persian, or from one of the Arabian or eastern African countries.

The woman looked down at Steve. "Do you know where your neighbors, the Porters, are? I need to thank Bob for his kindness and forgiveness."

Bob overheard the woman's voice from the living room. He walked into view. "I'm Bob, on the other end of the foyer. Can I help you?"

"May I come in?" she asked.

Steve welcomed her, and she walked over to Bob. She took off her scarf, revealing a striking face with half-moon cheeks, focused but soft green eyes, and blonde hair that fell down both sides of her face to her chest. Only the blonde hair was missing. The woman before him covered a shaved head with the scarf, but the face? He would never forget it.

A chill ran up Bob's spine "Abigail? What are you doing here? The —" Then he remembered his comments to the others earlier. "Big surprise, I've gotta say."

As Abigail followed Bob into the living room, gasps and hushes arose from the gathering. They'd also overheard the conversation at the door, the foyer carrying their voices. "My goodness, we were just talking about you.

Are you dressed this way because you feel threatened?" Betty asked.

"I had to become someone else, or I knew I would not live, so I had to disappear to stay alive," she said. "After my confession."

Steve stepped up to her. "I'm Steve Carter, the owner of this house. Like Betty said, we were just talking about somehow locating you, reaching out, seeing if you were okay, and inviting you in for a little safety." He looked at Annie, who nodded. "Abigail, Annie and I want to invite you to stay in our home. You are more than welcome. We have a lot of extra bedrooms."

"This is your house, Annie Carter?" Abigail asked, her wide-open eyes taking in the stunning scene.

"I'm one of those lucky girls with a five-star husband," she said quietly, stepping behind Steve and wrapping her arms around him as she addressed Abigail from over Steve's shoulder.

Abigail sat down on the floor with her head bowed. She started to cry, and the room went very quiet. "God is having mercy on me. I was doing such an evil thing, but Bob forgave me, and now God must be forgiving me, too."

"But," Bob replied, "you're safe now and you are part of our 'family'. You can make a new life with all of us, if you so desire. Welcome."

CHAPTER

13

OH NO, NOT ANOTHER EVIL PLOT

Soapy struggled mightily with the reversed fortunes of the Tough Guys. A rival organization to MWT just a couple months ago, TG's popularity was now leaking like a sieve. Recruitments were down, some were leaving, while across town, Bob's MWT was doing great. At their weekly staff meeting, Rusty reported that TG's spies had been watching Bob at his home. But they also were very sure he regularly visited his neighbors, Annie and Steve Carter, "in one of the city's finest residences; I'd love those 400 acres or so he's got," Rusty added.

More importantly, the spies were convinced of considerable activity and planning that was underway at the mansion. Many were now living there, the four-person Carter family plus perhaps a half dozen others. The spy committee's assessment was that everyone underneath the roof was a critical member of MWT, well-connected and hard-working and contributing strongly to its success. They were probably helping MWT plan a strategy to help the organization grow and influence society even further, from one coast to the other. "Several huge women appear to be living there, too," Rusty added. "Too bad there isn't a big tornado heading for that mansion. That would solve our problems."

"Tornados aren't the only powerful things in the world," Soapy said.

The staff grew quiet. The meeting soon ended, and everyone walked out without saying a word. But they looked at each other with grim, serious expressions on their faces, like they'd just stepped out of a war-torn forest.

Rusty made contact with Tony from the Mafia. "Are you aware of what's going on at the Carters' home?"

"Are you kidding? Of course, we know. We will handle it soon."

At the next weekly TG meeting, Rusty shared his conversation with Tony. Soapy was quiet. Everyone looked at each other and was afraid to comment. They all knew the Mafia was planning something, whether or not they wanted to participate. If they were to succeed, it certainly would benefit TG. But if the Mafia was acting, they were acting criminally. You could count on it. Could they live with the guilt for not reporting their suspicions to the police? Trying to set up a false scene with Abigail at the post office was a crime, but the Mafia's intentions for Bob and the group was an even deeper sin.

After a few minutes of silence, Soapy cleared his throat. "I can't condone violence to solve our problem.

Let's ponder this whole thing." But they all knew the longer they pondered, the more likely all hell would break loose.

At the next Mafia meeting, Boss Giovanni began putting together the master plan to eliminate MWT. "We know that the key members of the MWT movement are meeting several times a week at Steve Carters' huge mansion at 2150 Sunset Hill in Merrydale. We've been checking out the neighborhood, and the houses just recently built on his sprawling land, and one well-placed bomb can take out the Carter home and change the whole ball game. As before, we've found another radical nut who thinks our contact with him represents a religious terrorist group."

"Hopefully that radical nut is more efficient than that teenage clown Madido who botched a point-blank range chance to take this Porter down," one of the local bosses said. "How you blow it at twenty feet with a hand cannon is beyond me." He slapped his forehead. "Just make sure this next guy has a clue."

"We will, we will," Giovanni said, settling down the room by pushing his palms toward the ground. "Now to continue, next Thursday our hired gun, or bomber, will knock on the door at 6:30, the time their group gets together. He'll be delivering pizzas. Only the pizzas will be bombs. When the door opens, he'll rush in and blow himself up, along with everyone in the room.

"This will happen right after that group's ten-minute meditation, before supper. There should be fifteen people in the room. They'll be relaxed, calm, unsuspecting, you know, what we hope to get for an hour a week at Mass. Our plot will destroy the entire leadership of MWT and more. It will scare prospective members who are thinking of joining. And it could be the end of MWT.

"I caution you boys — it'll scare our wives, too," Giovanni continued. "I know many of you have complained how they aren't taking orders like they used to. I heard about what happened to you, Charlie, when you smacked your wife for not bringing in the dessert right away after dinner. Apparently, she hit you, which is why you have that black eye, right?"

"Yeah, but I'm not the only one being bullied by seven-foot-tall bitches."

Everyone yelled, "That's right, that's right!"

The meeting ended with everyone smacking each other's hand in high fives while yelling, "Hooray, hooray!"

After the ten-minute group meditation Steve announced he needed to talk about something important. "With all the anger that TG is expressing toward Bob and Annie for all their good work, I'm led to believe that for our own safety, we should be very alert," he said, his voice calm but etched with concern. "I know that the assassination attempt on you, Bob, has not been officially linked to the TGs, but they obviously were behind the infidelity scheme. If I'm correct, there is no question they will continue to try to destroy us, probably escalating the methods they use, since we're proving impossible to put down."

"I've been thinking about this, too," Bob said. "I'm not sure what we should do differently, because I think we all love what we've been doing, and it sorta takes us out of our unique approach to life to bring in guards around our 'church'."

"Oh Bob, I really understand your point of view, but besides being your second-in-command with MWG, let's not forget I'm a mother with a job at the paper, pretty exposed publicly every day, and I don't want my kids to get hurt," Annie added.

"Gotcha. Let's think about all this while we meditate."

The Mafia's plans were finalized. Tony passed the bomb on to Randy, the radical convert who would be posing as a pizza delivery driver. Randy was going to make his fake pizza delivery to the mansion, step inside, and Kaboom! How much easier could it be? The kid wanted his date with Allah and seventy-two virgins; he was committed. The mob painted "Perfect Pizza" in huge letters on each side of the van. The bomb was so big it had to be placed in three pizza boxes that were converted into one big box.

The evening after the Mafia planned their horrible act, their wives had assembled for their own weekly get together. Little did their husbands know what the eight women were discussing. They were putting together their own plan, not one their husbands were likely to back.

Margaret was the first to speak. "Well, girls, our efforts to find out what's going on at our silly husbands' meetings has paid off. Francesca told me what our dumb little midgets are up to. The guys don't realize Fran has been listening to them while she brings them coffee and donuts. They think she doesn't understand Italian because she's a Mexican, but she does. At my suggestion, she listened to their conversations at the door before she brought in the food. Also, she's tall enough to put her ears next to the heating vents, and she could hear what they were saying when she wasn't in the room. She's pretty sure she's got the whole picture."

"I'm so glad we got her to join us on our project," Bella added.

"On Thursday night, ladies, our husbands, or the latest misguided kid they've found to do the job, are planning to kill everyone involved in the MWT leadership. They are sending some radical nut with a bomb to that mansion where Bob Porter meets with his allies."

"Oh no!" Harriet, said.

"I – don't – think –so," another added, folding her arms tightly to her chest.

"What are we going to do?" Bella asked.

"I have come up with a plan, but we're going to need your help."

"Can't we just call the police?" Harriet asked.

"No," Margaret answered, "that would put our guys in jail, and then we wouldn't have the fun of ordering them around anymore or bopping them on the head when they get out of line...like they used to do to us.

"Here is the plan. It's a little complicated because we're going to have to deal with some mob spies who will be monitoring the bomb deliverer from a couple of different points. Anyway..."

CHAPTER

14

IT'S ABOUT TO HAPPEN

The Carters' mansion was bursting with music and joy, the kind that amplifies into its own feeling when sixteen people are participating in it. Laughter, a little dancing, light-hearted banter and compassion filled the room.

Which led Bob to become puzzled when he glanced out the living room window. He could barely believe his eyes. He turned to the others. "Look everyone! There are eight really tall apparently Muslim women parading back and forth in front of this place. They have signs that say 'Sign Up Now for The TGs'. Are they serious?"

"Should we call the police?" Jane asked.

"No, but let's hold off our meditation until they leave."

Just then, a pizza van arrived outside. When a nervous young man, really a boy, got out of the van and walked toward the mansion, balancing a huge pizza box on his hand like a well-skilled delivery man, two of the Muslim women grabbed him, took the pizza box away and shoved him back in the van. Two other ladies hopped in the van, closed the doors and drove off.

The remaining four Muslim women walked up to the Carters' front door. Steve opened it before they rang the bell, since everyone now stared out the windows, taking in the whole puzzling, baffling scene. Whatever it was, Steve sensed danger. He braced himself for whatever was coming next.

Steve stared at the ladies. "What's going on here? Who sent you to harass us? Why throw a delivery man in the van? You need to leave."

There was silence. Instead of answering him, the woman directly opposite Steve looked at her watch. She waited... for what? Was her watch broken? Steve wondered. A second later, a huge explosion blew through a large park on the northern side of the Carter properties. The park was created by Steve and Annie when they set up their unique housing development.

The woman turned and fixed her eyes down and onto Steve's. "That bomb you just heard explode was going to be detonated in your living room. It would have easily killed or maimed all of you. We warn you to guard yourselves."

The women turned around, ran, and jumped into an Uber that had just arrived.

A long meeting with the police followed at Steve's house. No one had any idea who the Muslim women were, why they were stopping an attempt to kill them, or who the bomber was. The van had disappeared in the explosion. The "family" realized they were in danger and needed protection. However, Bob was not happy with the police orders for police to guard the mansion twenty-four hours a day. To remedy that, the Neighborhood Association came up with a plan that Bob, Steve and the police agreed to.

At the next Neighborhood Association meeting, Bob explained the plan as he understood it, a plan endorsed by everyone in the room. "We all like to take walks in our own beautiful neighborhood that Steve and Annie created," Bob began. "So every day, let's have our big ladies and a couple small men circle the grounds. With all the ladies we've have here, each woman will only have to put in a couple of hours a week. And in spite of what that crazy Soapy doesn't want us to do, we can give them a gun or two.

No little guys are going to mess with our families. This will show our support for MWT."

The ensuing press and TV coverage of the escalating showdown between TGs and MWT, and MWT's overall success in positively affecting societies far and wide, helped spread the vision of MWT to value people for their spiritual qualities of courage, kindness and brother and sisterly love rather than their size, strength, race, gender, or religion."

This was not what TG and the Mafia were preaching.

When he learned of the latest botched hit attempt on Bob and his immediate MWT officers, Soapy was relieved it failed. Just as he'd been relieved when the other incompetent kid brought in by the Mafia, or a terrorist group, messed up his chance to shoot himself into smithereens. He began to realize that his desire to make TG succeed was not as strong as the feelings of guilt that would encompass him if Bob had been killed, even if not directly involved.

It was time to make a decision that was going to rock the nation. And infuriate a lot of men.

CHAPTER

15

I'M GETTING OUTTA HERE

Two days after the bomb plot failed, Soapy went on TV to announce that he was giving up the leadership of TG. "Violence is not the answer to the challenges our world faces," he said, his voice strong and resolute, the voice of a giant in corporate industry. "I still believe in some of the philosophy of TG but not all. And if TG inadvertently incites some people to consider violence as acceptable, I can no longer be a part of it."

Later, the President issued a statement at the White House briefing to commend Soapy's decision.

After the TV was turned off in the Carters' living room, Jane asked, "Would it be crazy to invite Soapy to join us some evening?"

"No, I think it's a good idea," Bob said. "He's not a bad guy. We even had a few nice words to say to each other while getting ready for our debate. And we all learn something when we spend time with people who don't agree with us. His comments about violence are what the whole world needs to consider. I say, let's get him to join the 'family'."

Meanwhile, the Mafia mob was in turmoil, their latest plans smashed to the ground by some mysterious Muslim women. The guys couldn't understand why their wives were smiling, and they never asked their husbands why they were so unhappy. They didn't seem to care.

"What happened to our great plot?" Giovanni asked. "Who sabotaged us? Who had the gall to sabotage us?"

One of the spies who witnessed the attempted bombing answered, "There were eight Muslim women dressed in black protesting outside the mansion with signs supporting TG—"

"No kidding, genius," Giovanni growled. "I heard about that last night after it happened. As you were saying?"

"We left them alone because they seemed to be on our side, at the very least distractions to the people inside so we could get Randy and the pizza box up to the door. Instead, those women were traitors. When Randy arrived, the Muslims grabbed him and the bomb, stole the van with him in the back and drove off. Ten minutes later, they blew up the bomb in a nearby park. The whole plan was a complete failure. Somebody must have known what was going to happen. There must be some spies within this room."

Just then the door to the mob meeting room burst open and the eight wives rushed into the room, looking like a fearsome defensive line about to smash the quarterback. "Okay, you little jerks," Margaret declared, "You are going to listen to us. The mob is finished."

"Are you kidding? Get outta here, woman. You're out of place!" Giovanni snarled at his wife.

One of the larger wives, Suzanne, grabbed Giovanni by the seat of his pants and threw him against the wall. Then she turned him around and held him up close to the ceiling by his throat.

"Wait!" Margaret shouted. "That's my husband. Let me hold him up there."

Then she took over. While a pinned Giovanni listened helplessly, she turned to the room. "Okay, men, here is the plan. The mob is finished. We stopped your horrible assassination attempt, the eight of us, your own wives who unlike you value human life, and now we're going to give you the opportunity to change all our lives."

The men sat in stone silence as they peered up at their scary Amazonian wives, their lifelong vows of submission as Mafiosa now as far away from the moment as a distant galaxy.

"We've found something wonderful that you're going to do instead of beating people up, selling drugs and threatening people," Margaret said. "We learned the local university needs a good Italian teacher. So, Benito, you will be hired by them next semester. I've already arranged it, they already have your CV. Done."

She squeezed Giovanni's neck for effect. "Ash... ash..." Giovanni gasped.

"And as for you, Henry, you're a computer whiz and

have been doing the IT work and social communication for the mob, so we have found a small company that needs your skills."

Margaret let Giovanni down. He grasped his neck and shot her a look that could kill a bull elephant. She snickered, the best new adventure of all coming to mind.

"This town has only one small lousy Italian restaurant--the crappy little place where you have your meetings. You have been complaining about this for years. So, the rest of you are going to start a bigger and better Italian restaurant here in Merrydale. Most of you will cook while we help you get started."

"Are you nuts?" Giovanni yelled. "You can't make us do that."

"Sure we can, honey." Margaret and the other seven wives strode over to their husbands, dropped them on the floor and sat on them. Quickly, they realized there was not going to be any more discussion...it was a done deal.

A while later at one of their weekly "family" get- togethers, Bob mentioned, "Did you know we finally have a great Italian restaurant in town? And they deliver, too. Wouldn't it be terrific if we had some delicious pasta instead of our barbecued chicken every so often? And it doesn't have that seedy back room feel the other place started getting when Tony and his Mafia friends started meeting there."

"Yes, it's a terrific restaurant, and I'm writing an article for the paper about them," Annie said.

"Have you also noticed the local paper reports that crime seems to have decreased?" Steve asked. "Wouldn't it be funny if the families running the restaurant were mafia guys who now have better jobs?"

Everyone laughed. Jane said, "Come on now, don't be silly."

Soapy, who was attending the "family" gathering for the first time, felt really uncomfortable. He felt he couldn't tell everybody what he knew, or at least suspected, but something urged him to comment, "Nothing is impossible."

"Oh yes it is, Soapy. It's impossible for you to beat me at Scrabble," Bob joked.

And so the Scrabble games started. With so many people in the "family" now, they had to set up three boards. "Dessert and Scrabble with friends, what could be better?" Annie said with a smile.

Barbara and Betty continued to see Madido every week. His happiness grew with each visit, now palpable when they arrived. After a few months the change in Madido was evident — he had connected with his heart. Bob, Steve, Barbara and Betty went to the District Attorney to see if there was any possibility to release him on bail if he would reveal who set him up to assassinate Bob.

"Madido has changed dramatically," Steve said to the D.A.

His trial had not yet occurred, due to all kinds of emerging issues. And questions? Was he sane at the time of the attempt? Was he sane now? Did he act alone?

If not, why was he not coming forth and identifying the people who put him up to it? "He does that, and I think we have something to talk about," the DA emphasized.

Legal matters in the case were complicated, and both his defense lawyers and the prosecuting attorneys were laboring long and hard preparing for the upcoming trial.

The D.A. agreed if Madido gave them information, he would consider releasing him to the custody of Steve Carter, where he would take up supervised residence. Steve was a lawyer and was once a police officer; he still had his credentials. Since Madido was only nineteen at the time of the incident, the D.A. felt compassion for him when the girls who had whisked the violently angry man out of the auditorium told him he barely resembled the would-be assassin in physical appearance anymore.

On the next visit to the jail, Bob and the ladies finally raised the crucial question. "Madido, were you ever encouraged to try to assassinate Bob?"

"I can't say."

"Well, son, I think you might want to say. Because if you do, the D.A.'s considering releasing you on bail."

MA dido's eyes brightened. "Where would I go?"

"You let us worry about that."

Madido looked over to Barbara and Betty, both of whom nodded their heads. Tell him, Madido.

"Yes, I was approached by someone who claimed he was a terrorist. I had a lot of calls and emails from people in the Middle East, after I had subscribed to a radical website and became sympathetic to them. I was so depressed and felt no self-worth, and they started to give me purpose in life. Only now I can see what a horrible purpose it was.

"I met a young man at Starbucks one day who noticed how depressed I was. He sensed that I needed purpose. I didn't want to live, and the idea of becoming a martyr for radical terrorists really hooked me. And having seventy-two virgins in heaven sounded pretty good too." He chuckled nervously.

"Who was the young man, Madido?"

"He told me his name was Ronald Barnes. I'm guessing it was a fake name. After he gave me the gun, I never saw him again. Before I was found and arrested, I went back to Starbucks many times with a scarf around my face, but I never saw him again."

Bob went to the D.A. with the latest information. Days later, Madido was secretly and quietly released to the custody of Steve and Annie. Madido was included in all the gatherings, and his whole approach to life transformed when he looked around the room and took in the joy, the smiles, and the laughs. He was in heaven, as much as one on earth could be. He couldn't imagine a better moment, with many more to come in his new, more self-assured and spiritual life.

CHAPTER

16

AGAIN?
ARE YOU KIDDING?

While watching *Downton Abby* after Sunday dinner, Bob, Jane, Steve, Annie, Barbara, Betty, Abigail and Madido heard a knock on the door. Steve opened it and found himself face-to-face with their neighbor, Fred, who cast a blank, puzzled stare. His face looked like a merger of a smile and impending gloom.

"What's up?" Steve asked.

"The sphere is returning. The scientists say it might make women go back to their original size."

"Oh, come in," Jane said. "Tell us what you heard. We've been streaming *Downton Abby* so we didn't see the news. That's unbelievable, just as unbelievable as what happened to us two years ago! What does everyone think?"

Annie spoke first. "Oh, I'm so happy that I might get to downsize and be who I really am again!"

"Not me," Jane laughed. "I love being stronger than Bob."

Steve joked, "Me neither. I loved having Annie open doors for me, and I hate to admit it, but I'm also into her ultra-long legs."

"I think this whole experience has taught us so much," Bob said, bringing some focus on the moment. "It's made us see each other differently. Instead of focusing on physical bodies, we've checked out our spiritual qualities. And if we didn't do that, we were in trouble... like I was when this whole thing first happened. I had to change the way I looked at the world, at others, as well as myself."

"Well, it really did shake up the world," Steve added. "Do you think when women go back to their 'normal' sizes, some of the good things people learned from the sphere's visit will stay with us?"

"Some have learned and won't go back to their old ways of thinking," Jane said. She looked over at Bob. "I've never said it before, but Bob was always great the way he was able to be great then. But treating me right was not one of those things. Even though I loved him deeply, he always intimidated me. Now he doesn't. I know with all my heart that Bob will treat me as he does now, even if I do return to my smaller size. I think he's learned more than most of us."

"Yes, I did learn. But I believe the most important thing I learned was humility," Bob said.

"That's funny," Annie said. "Humility wasn't the most important thing I had to learn."

Steve laughed. "That's true, you were always the most humble." He added softly, "And the most beautiful woman I'd ever met... other than Jane, Betty and Barbara."

Everyone laughed as Steve continued "Your only problem was you never stuck up for yourself. I had to keep drawing you out. You didn't have to be pushy, just honest. I think women are going to have to start speaking up for themselves."

"I know, I know," Annie agreed, "and this whole mess got me thinking that all women need to speak up more. Before we grew so large this was not an easy thing to do. Jane, can I tell what happened to us earlier in our lives?"

Jane sighed, "Yes."

"Jane was beaten by her first husband, and I was raped as a teenager. When I worked at a TV station as a correspondent, my boss threatened to fire me if I didn't have sex with him. So I was fired. Jane's first husband only agreed to a divorce on the condition she didn't tell anyone about his abuse. And I didn't tell anyone what happened to me. But maybe we have to change this mindset, though that's not easy. I felt so guilty and dirty after I was raped. I wanted so badly to forget it. Telling anyone seemed like it would make me feel even worse."

Jane nodded her head and moved next to Annie. "I know how you felt, too. I thought I had done something so wrong that Ted was justified hitting me. I guess I was kinda stupid. I just didn't want anyone to know what was going on in our home."

"I know this is a shock to all of you," Annie added.

"But if all women who were physically abused or sexually assaulted had reported the crime, I bet a lot of men might have thought twice before they did something like that. Steve, you never pushed me around. You were always gentle and kind, a real man. But while working with our MWT, I saw many women who had been treated badly by men, often their husbands or coworkers or bosses. So now that women have become the physically bigger people, men are encouraged to communicate, rather than push us down as some did when we were smaller."

Then Bob cried out, "Oh, Lord help us. Jane, why didn't you ever tell me about this?"

"Because we needed to move forward in our own lives, and I was desperate to put it behind me. When I met you, that was my chance. So I did."

Annie added, "Of course we should have reported what happened immediately, as all women should do today. But as Jane said, we must move forward now and put these things behind us...we must forget these horrors ever happened and know our purity has never been taken from us."

"In the future, the women's movements growing all over the country should switch from being activist to great support groups for women everywhere. Then we know that we have harmony with men in society. Sometimes in the past, when a brave woman did report what was done to her, she was ignored. But now when women report crimes, like those done to Annie and me, they won't be alone anymore. I believe I heard a senator once indicated that women will soon have collective power because of the women's movements. Together with other women, they will be able to speak without fear."

Everyone agreed, nodding their heads. "Thank God I never, had to endure what Annie and Jane did," Betty said. "But so often at work, I witnessed some of my colleagues treated disrespectfully by their male bosses. I learned some, were forced by their bosses to have sex with them. I'm so ashamed and sorry I never reported what I witnessed. I think I knew I'd lose my job if I spoke up."

"Maybe because I was an young executive with our business—"

"I thought you were in your early twenties," Madido said, his eyes raising in surprise.

"Late twenties... thank you for the compliment, you sweet man." Barbara turned to Betty, who started laughing. "We're a year apart, but we love your calendar, Madido."

Barbara turned back to the others. "I didn't have to endure much pressure from my subordinates, but sometimes I just couldn't stand the way they spoke to me. After I gave them some directions as to what their daily assignments were some would say, 'yes, princess.' I don't think they realized how that made me feel."

Steve took in the conversation, then recalled an incident in his law firm.

"Oh, my goodness, I have to confess that, many,

many years ago, when I started working at my law firm, I used that expression with a female partner and boy, did she let me have it," he confessed. "I learned then and there not to take that approach again. Ha, I've been a good boy since then."

Everybody laughed. Annie playfully slapped him. "Hey, now that you women are all taller and stronger than us men, maybe you should take over...be the bosses," Steve concluded.

"Oh, come on, it's not about being bosses. We just wanted to be treated equally, respectfully," Annie said. "You men think of power, being the boss, having control. We think of all of us sharing that power, that supervision, that control."

"I think women rising and having an equal voice just might make a great difference in the world. Fewer wars, more cooperation, more compassion, more caring," Jane said.

Bob scratched his trimmed beard. "Well, I guess we all have things to learn. Forgive me for changing the subject, but I wonder how the rest of you feel about the return of the sphere and what the future might have in store for us."

Madido spoke first. "I don't know what to think about the future, but I certainly am grateful for the sphere's first visit. It made me mad, I did something really stupid—, "he looked up, "I'm so sorry again, Mr. Porter. Then the miracle of you and Barbara and Betty changed my life. I'm actually happy now, happy most of the time, not always feeling like I have nowhere to go."

Madido turned to Steve. "If I had not met you, Mr. Carter, I would have never had any interest in the law. By letting me assist you in your office, you got me interested in going back to school if I ever get out of this mess. And the willingness of some of you to contribute to my tuition — well, what can I ever do to repay you? I'm so glad that sphere came and that I've changed. I can deal with my life now."

Barbara and Betty smiled, delighted by Madido's words.

A question-and-answer session broke out. When was the sphere coming back? Would it really return women to their former sizes? What was in the future for everyone? Would all hell break loose again?

The news about the predicted return of the sphere shook the planet. The clothing industry would boom again because sales would skyrocket. Barbie dolls might reappear in the toy stores. The Lakers, on the other hand, would be dismayed because Rachel Good, their eight-foot-tall superstar, might shrink to her previous 6'4" size, not good enough to keep her in the NBA. The women's team owners were ecstatic. Their stars might be coming back after two very lean seasons.

Some Middle Eastern men equally rejoiced, celebrating the return to order, which in the home meant ordering around their wives again. But they kept it to themselves. Many ladies were sad they wouldn't have beautiful gigantic legs to show off, and the men felt just the same. But they kept quiet.

The big question was still, when would it happen?

The scientists couldn't predict an exact date. Their best guess was two or three months. That remained to be seen.

The next morning at Folcano's Restaurant, the mobsters and their wives had breakfast before planning the rest of the day. The guys were laughing and excited that they again might be taller than their wives. The wives, however, had mixed feelings about the predictions for their future. One guy shouted, "We can go back to being real mobsters again."

While the men all laughed, the ladies scowled art them. "Look you dummies, we aren't there yet, and if you aren't careful, we'll grab you and lock you up," Margaret said. More laughter followed.

Giovanni jumped in, "Listen everybody. Bob Porter and his 'family' made reservations for next Tuesday night. This will make us famous. Forget the mob stuff. This is much better than our old world."

They all stood and jubilantly raised their glasses of orange juice in a toast to the future. "And ladies, I'm gonna promise that we'll work together as equals, even when you go back to being midgets, 'cause you were the ones who came up with the great restaurant idea. It's so much more fun than selling drugs. We owe it to you. And we're not using the 'F' word anymore."

Everybody was happy and started exchanging hugs, and they just couldn't wait for the following Tuesday to come, when a panel of some of the world's most prominent scientists would debate the return of the sphere. Every major network planned to carry the debate.

Unfortunately, the news was a bit unsettling. Much of the country was glued to the TV for the debate and what possible effects it would have on the earth's inhabitants. Were the women going to grow even taller, or were they going to go back to their original size? Would the men shrink further, to give the women even more physical authority? The scientists were at least able to agree that the sphere would be back in approximately two months.

The next day, all hell broke loose around the country. Sports teams weren't sure what to do. So many had hired huge women and wondered how they could get out of their contracts if the new teammates went back to being smaller. Or what if they grew even larger? The women were upset because they had no idea what would happen to them. Of course, the men didn't know what to expect, either.

Realizing the turmoil sweeping the nation, and knowing he alone could not calm the people, the President invited Bob and Annie to address the nation.

"My fellow Americans, it is with deep gratitude that I introduce to you Bob Porter and Annie Carter, who have graciously agreed to offer some of their insights regarding the challenging times we face," the President began. "We have endured more than two years of one of the greatest challenges in our history, one tougher than COVID, and I am so proud of this nation. During that time, you have strived valiantly to comfort one another, even in the midst of your own fears.

"In spite of the turmoil created by the sphere that circled our world, we have seen incredible improvements in many areas of our nation. Domestic abuse statistics have declined dramatically. Equal pay for equal work among women is becoming the norm. Sexual harassment of all kinds is declining, and in fact has practically ceased.

"There have been numerous social improvements in many countries around the world," the President continued. "Forced marriages for eleven-year-old girls, many close to seven feet tall, has ceased. Women's rights have increased dramatically. In short, we are making it through this crisis.

"The secret to our survival has been compassion and love for each other. Now, with the unknown effects coming soon with the sphere's reappearance, we must join together and have confidence that we can face whatever challenges are presented. And now, Bob and Annie, will you be so kind as to help us prepare for whatever the future may bring?"

Bob let Annie step up to the podium first. She pulled out a single sheet of bullet points she'd made, but her eyes were focused directly on the camera. She wasn't using a teleprompter. She adjusted the microphone upward from the President's height.

"Women, even if we go back to our former size, we will have grown in our understanding of life and in the way we should really view ourselves and others. Let's look at ourselves as wonderful creations of the good Lord, both men and women, with qualities of tenderness, warmth, goodness and kindness, and not just as physical beings. We all have feminine and masculine qualities, and that makes us one. If we must grow taller still, we can handle it just as we have handled what we have already endured. If we go back to our original sizes, many of us will be very grateful and will appreciate all we have learned from this experience. And heaven help us if we do get bigger, let's continue to refrain from taking revenge on the men who mistreated us when we were smaller than them. Continue to forgive, and trust men will be touched by our understanding.

"I once learned the Prayer of St. Francis, that began 'Lord, make me an instrument of thy peace; where there is hatred let me sow love, where there is injury, pardon...' Maybe we should all remember those words," Annie added.

After Annie sat down, Bob addressed the throng of reporters in the White House briefing room as the nation watched riveted to the TV. "Annie has made some wonderful points. We men have also learned much from this experience. I think we are more aware of what women have had to endure now that we've walked in their shoes for a while. Because of the sphere, men have had similar experiences and can see who we really are. We must be comforting, respectful and supportive to the wonderful women in our lives. So many of us have learned to appreciate how women protect us, not the other way around. The bottom line, I think, is we have learned to view each other more spiritually than physically from this strange experience. Mr. President?"

The President shook Bob's hand as he headed back to the podium.

"Ladies and gentlemen, let us comfort and support each other during the next months as we await the return of the sphere," the President said, a soothing grin on his face. "When it arrives, know that no matter how it affects us, it cannot break us apart. We are one, man and woman, woman and man. The value of human life knows no gender. This is true for intellectual, as well as physical and spiritual, abilities of men and women.

"I would like to finish with an excerpt from a speech given by Michelle Obama to a group called Let Girls Learn, concerning intellectual equality for women. She said: 'The more I traveled and met with girls and learned from experts...the more I realized that the barriers to girls' education aren't just resources. It's not just about access to scholarships or transportation or school bathrooms. It's also about attitudes and beliefs—that girls simply aren't worthy of an education; that women should have no role outside the home; that their bodies aren't their own...'

"In addition, UN studies have shown that allowing girls to get an education in countries such as Pakistan is a plus for the world's economy. It will increase and be key to ensuring global prosperity. I believe this is a very important aspect of our goal to promote peace between men and women at this historic time."

The address did as it intended, temporarily soothing the frayed nerves of the nation while providing more information and ways to manage lives and emotions through whatever turmoil followed the sphere's next visit. Still, the question that remained on everyone's mind: "What is the sphere going to do to us this time?"

At the weekly "family" gathering Abigail, along with all the others, congratulated Annie and Bob for their inspiring messages. "I'm so grateful that we have our 'family' here. Annie and Steve, we really appreciate your kindness inviting all of us to your lovely home. And now, as 'family', let us lock arms together and know that no matter what the future brings, we will survive. "Bob, you have taught us so much. You've taught us that each one of us can really change for the better."

"Thanks for your kind words, Abigail. Actually, so many of us have gone through change, both in our thinking and in our sizes. Our changes have made all of us better people. So let's know that whatever the sphere showers on us, it will be an opportunity for us to grow more...to make even more progress. We're stronger than any sphere."

"Yes, we are!" One of the family members yelled. More hoots and cheers followed.

The wonderful peace the "family" enjoyed was not typical in the rest of the country, or the world for that matter. Many men worried matters would get even worse for them. And some women were afraid forced or arranged marriages would start again if they shrunk back to normal. Those women had enjoyed being able to call the shots for the last couple of years. So while they were still able to speak up, they tried to get the message out: "Hey, let's change things permanently, no matter what happens."

Since no one knew what to expect, negotiations were in process all over the world. Men and women were both offered deals. Lawyers were busier than ever before in history. If nothing else happened, Steve thought as he mulled over these domestic and international legal challenges, at least most men recognized women's strength, not only physically, but their spiritual strength and the strength of their wisdom. "What if" was the beginning of all negotiations. Much of the communication would not have happened at all if everybody knew what was going to occur in two months.

But the sphere knew, and she was going to surprise everyone.

CHAPTER

17

NOW THEY HAVE
A REAL CHALLENGE

Two months of uncertainty passed, the entire world on pins and needles, the sphere's arrival expected any time. Most people didn't want anything else to happen. Everyone worried that the women would grow even taller. Even though the height advantage had caused men to be nicer to them, most women didn't want to grow any bigger. A poll taken by CBS News showed that most would like to revert to a size between their current heights and those of men.

All the "family" members prayed day and night to understand that the good Lord was in control of the situation. Bob assured everyone at the regular "family" get-together that everything would be all right. "Look how far we've come. So many of us were on different sides of the river, and just look how we've come together. That wonderful quote from the Bible, '...all things work together for good to them that love God...' sure has been true for us. No matter what happens, we'll stick together and help others deal with the situation regardless how it turns out. Hey, let's take a look at the latest news!"

And then it happened.

The sphere arrived in the middle of the night above the U.S. and circled the globe four times. After it left, people started asking each other, "Do you feel anything?" Everyone was again in a state of high anxiety as scientists tried to determine how the vibrations cascading down to earth were going to affect the planet's populace.

After a week of nervous waiting, men began to notice changes happening to some of them, but not all. Some men grew taller, a situation as puzzling as that which occurred when the sphere visited earlier. Why weren't all men getting taller like the women did in the earlier event?

Scientists and doctors examined a large sample of men, both those who grew taller and those who didn't, to determine the difference. After a month of round-the-clock research, no one was able to come up with an explanation for this strange phenomenon. The word on everyone's lips was, "Why?"

At the next "family" meeting, everyone gathered after supper in the grand living room. They watched a TV discussion among men who had not grown taller, and men who had. About a half-hour into the program, Bob picked up something. "Has anyone noticed anything different between the tall men and the 'normal' ones? And why are all the men in our 'family' growing taller?"

"No, I didn't notice anything except that maybe the

taller ones seem a little softer spoken. Maybe their growth has affected their vocal cords?" Steve said.

"Maybe the bigger men are more humble," Abigail suggested.

Betty added, "Well, at least they don't scare me anymore, even if they are bigger."

"The big men seem kinda nice. At least the ones I know. I wish my dad had been more like them," Madido said.

Bob smiled. "I think y'all have hit the nail on the head. It appears to me that there's a huge psychological difference between the men not affected by the rays and those who were, no matter what their original size. It's possible that those growing taller have quieted down because they're troubled by their new size, but I'm not sure."

Bob asked Steve, Madido and Soapy, "Does the fact that you are growing so much taller trouble you?"

"No," they all answered.

"Well, I'm going to call MSNBC and ask them to have a psychologist interview a hundred men, fifty big and fifty normal sized. I have a suspicion that mental and emotional maturity, and the way they treat women, may have something to do with this phenomenon."

A few weeks later, a news broadcast revealed results of the study, which determined rays from the sphere only affected men who had a sense of humility. That slower, gentler mental state relaxed their genes, so the rays were free to make them grow. Incredibly, two men from the group of smaller men who apologized to the psychologist for their rudeness started to grow three days later. Their apology wasn't offered because they wanted to grow, but because they were sincerely sorry, ashamed and embarrassed that frustration got the best of them.

The first stage of humility had occurred. The experts determined that humility, which fosters love, was the only way the rays could affect men's chromosomes, making some taller than women, just as they had been before. Relative heights were becoming as similar as they were prior to the sphere's first appearance.

As some men grew taller, those who didn't were not happy. Six months after the sphere's return, the relative size of women to men, who expressed humility, kindness and warmth, was just as it had been before the sphere's initial appearance. But many people were now larger than their previous size before the sphere's first visit.

Men who hadn't changed from their original size before the first sphere visit were furious and wrestled with their dilemma. Why didn't this humility thing happen to the women? Many tall women had absolutely no humility, were pushy and complete egotists...they should never have grown taller. What was the answer?

As it turned out, the answer to that question was just around the corner.

A year passed without another return of the sphere. Changes began occurring on every continent. It was a slow process, but many men and women began to talk to one another with more respect that anyone had thought possible. More men were losing their urge to be bossy. Brash and insensitive arrogance was not tolerated.

Women now had to deal with something else as well—the need for humility. It was apparently the correct order of things. First the sphere enlarged all women, because they already possessed humility from millennia being treated as inferiors by men. Now they required a deeper humility in order to maintain their bigger size.

Perhaps this was the best way for women to learn lessons, Annie thought. First, men had to deal with their character. Now it was time for women to learn a little more humility. Some were furious, because those who had been aggressive and arrogant began to shrink. Others thought it was ridiculous, claiming that they were humble enough already. Apparently, the sphere's rays didn't agree with them.

The latest phenomenon began to affect the dating game. Tall men and women knew a big date was a sure bet. At first small men, and now again small women, who didn't want to give up their big egos complained, "Look, I'm great, and that guy thinks he's great, too. So why can't we have a good time bossing each other around?"

Marriage was a little more complicated. When a little husband yelled and bullied his seven-foot wife, she might tenderly pick him up and lock him in the bathroom like a child. "When you feel like calming down, little one, I'll be happy to let you out." Or, when a giant humble husband was cruelly berated by his tiny wife, he might smile and remain quiet. He certainly didn't want to start shrinking!

But the world began to realize humility wasn't something you could just turn on and off. It had to be real, and it wasn't that easy to attain. Therapists, preachers, psychologists and counselors made fortunes. Their clients wanted to grow physically, but not necessarily spiritually, so hypocrisy wasn't working for them. Hypocrites didn't grow physically or spiritually. Authors published books dealing with humility, and the bookstores couldn't keep up with the demand.

Some people didn't know what humility was, or how to get it. However, scientific evidence proved that whatever it was, it was helping people to grow stronger. The message spread more and more effectively. People began to realize that if they were humble, they could maintain their oversized bodies, or grow from their relatively diminutive size. They would return to their previous heights as they were before the first sphere encounter. But if they didn't have true humility, the growth rays from the sphere held no effect on them.

All the small men and shrinking women were desperate to understand what humility was and how they could get it. "We need it. We want it," they all cried. "We want to stand tall and be up there with everyone else."

Then one day, scientists announced they had finally discovered the secret to gaining humility.

CHAPTER

18

THE SECRET IS OUT

The Carters, Porters and entire "family" gathered excitedly, as a special program was about to appear on TV. After dinner, they took their places on the big sofas and chairs surrounding the huge TV screen and settled in, their enjoyment in fellowship and being together quite palpable.

The President strolled into the White House briefing room, his stride resolute and sure, followed by professors and acclaimed psychologists from leading universities. They were joined by religious leaders from every denomination.

The living room grew quiet.

"Fellow Americans and citizens of the world," the President began, "we are here tonight to tell you what may be one of the most important scientific discoveries of all time. As we all know, our world has had two unusual encounters with a strange sphere in the past three years, which has affected mankind in a variety of ways, most of them substantial. Although these encounters have presented many challenges, we have also learned much from them.

"Before we share the latest discovery made by these esteemed scientists, psychologists and religious leaders, I will remind you all of the most important information that was discovered last year. Researchers discovered that humility was the only human quality needed to enable the sphere's rays to affect one's growth. Humility was the one quality necessary to take advantage of the strange vibrations and to prevent a reversal of growth.

"But how do we attain humility? That was the one question we were all asking, and we believe we finally have the answer."

The President paused and turned to the dignitaries standing behind him on the stage. With one voice, the entire group softly said two words: "Unselfish Love." They repeated those words over and over with great reverence, like a mantra, like a choir chanting a familiar hymn. The effect on the audience was magical. People worldwide sighed and smiled.

"Isn't this incredible?" The President continued. "If we want to gain humility, we must love others as ourselves. Even put others before ourselves. If we do that, we'll grow in so many ways. We will grow spiritually, and physically we will grow to the normal relative sizes we were before the sphere's visit." Bob and the "family" applauded loudly. "And if you are already at the standard size, you won't shrink." More applause.

"Remember what the Bible says in 1 Corinthians,

'Now abideth faith, hope, love, these three; but the greatest of these is love'."

The President walked back to the podium and took the glass of water sitting atop it — "that's pure rosewood," Bob said to everyone in the room — drank the entire glass, then began pacing the floor again.

"So, if we love our neighbor, our boss, our mate and even those who aren't so easy to love, our physical size will either remain or it will return to what is our normal relative size to all those who have gained true humility. If we find ourselves shrinking all we have to do is love everyone. And as I said before, love will make us grow in so many ways.

"Just think. If everyone put others before themselves, then everyone would have humility and love would take over, wars would cease, crime would disappear, injustice would evaporate, and lawyers would have to find another profession! It would be a much better life to live on this earth. We all need to know that all good is possible."

When the President finished, one religious leader stepped forward. "All of us standing here tonight agree that unselfish love is the core of all our religions," he said. "These sphere visits have made us examine ourselves. So on behalf of my colleagues, to all of you listening tonight, know that you can be the salt of the earth. Love others so you can develop humility and become the exact perfect size, and you will inspire others. As James said, 'Humble yourselves in the sight of the Lord and He shall lift you up'. When we love God first and have the humility to recognize the Lord as supreme, totally good and loving us unconditionally, we find that we will be loving others more."

With that the broadcast ended, with everyone shaking hands and hugging each other. Viewers all over the country went to bed that night pondering what they had heard. Would the world get the message?

At the next gathering, Bob suggested that instead of watching TV after dinner, they get together to talk about love. Everyone agreed and was enthusiastic about discussing the concept.

Steve started the discussion with a declaration. "Well, whatever love is, we all seem to be expressing it. Everyone in this room seems to be the proper size relative to what we were before the sphere's visit. I guess we are all fairly humble, and we certainly seem to express it by loving each other. But not all men and women around the world have figured that out yet."

Abigail spoke up. "Bob, you certainly expressed love when you forgave me for my stupid act."

"And I think you expressed even more love and humility by confessing you were a part of that deceptive scheme," Bob replied.

"I guess humility is also accepting that you might have done something wrong," Soapy said, thinking of his own mistakes, and those horrible judgments made by men purportedly carrying out his wishes for TG. "Confess it and then, most importantly, don't repeat that mistake."

"So just what is love?" Barbara asked rhetorically.

"Hey, let's play a game. Everyone gets a point for coming up with one quality of love, okay? Who wants to keep score?"

Madido shouted, "I will!" The words, "tenderness," "respect," "honor," "comfort," "unselfishness," and many others were shouted all at once.

"Hey, wait a minute. I can't keep score if you all shout at once," Madido smiled. Annie eventually won by putting down the greatest number of words.

There was no question the world was affected by all the information spread across the continents. Nations communicated with each other in much friendlier ways. Tensions eased and some wars ended. Divorces in the U.S. declined from 60% to 8% of new marriages, and they even dropped among long-term marriages that had failed in the past. Why? Divorced husbands and wives were finding their ways back to each other, the arguments and differences that pushed them apart no longer so relevant. Political campaigns were far more civil. Drug use decreased as happiness and pleasure came from the "high" of friendship, rather than chemical substances. Robberies decreased and religious radicalism slowly tapered off. Prejudice faded.

Things looked good. More and more people smiled at each other, and the few remaining proportionately shorter women and men were greeted with hugs and smiles. Soon, they started to smile back at people, and they began to grow back to the new normal proportions. The clothing industry was still the best investment.

Then the next stage of the lesson from the sphere presented itself.

CHAPTER

19

WHEN ON EARTH IS THIS GOING TO STOP?

Another sphere raced toward the earth. People were shocked and cried, "Help us, good Lord!" in every language around the world. "After all the progress we have made, why another visit from the sphere?"

Many religious leaders told their congregations not to worry and to remember the verse from 1 Corinthians: "By the grace of God I am what I am: and his grace which was bestowed upon me was not in vain."

"This experience will not make any important change in our lives," clergymen in churches throughout the country told their congregations more-or-less. "We've learned so much from these spheres. How to have humility. How to love. How to end war. Perhaps the good Lord is sending us a new experience to teach us even more."

Scientists and psychologists, however, were not

going down that path. They wouldn't believe anything that couldn't be supported by physical evidence.

Bob asked the "family" to sit together, grow quiet and pray. They started by holding hands, then sat back and were still. Soapy made only one comment. "Family," he said, "this fits perfectly with that quote from the Bible, 'Be still and know that I am God'." They all remained still for an hour.

Then they hugged each other, got out their Scrabble boards and quietly played. They didn't stay up late, because the sphere was predicted to arrive early, and they wanted to be awake when it appeared. But before going to bed, they took a moment to admire the beautiful full moon shining in a clear blue sky.

The next day, the world was quiet. Everyone looked toward the skies in silent anticipation of what was to come. Whether it was 3 a.m. or 2 a.m. or 7 p.m., it didn't matter. Wherever people were on earth it was their duty to watch and pray. Finally it came.

Just as before, the sphere again circled the earth. All military personnel put down their weapons while remaining on heightened alert in case of chaotic reactions. After the sphere left, the whole world remained quiet. Everyone looked at each other to see if anything was happening. They did this even though scientists predicted it would probably take a week for any changes to take effect.

True to those predictions, one week after the sphere's spin around the earth, it began to happen. At first it wasn't clear exactly what effects the sphere's visit had produced. Human bodies seemed to be growing in many different shapes, sizes and directions. But the result? Everyone was returning to original size. Some naturally tall women were much smaller than they were for the past few years, their size now back to pre-sphere levels.

Soon everyone sensed what was happening.

Little by little, civilization began to rejoice over its new condition. Sure, it had been fun for many women to be so tall that they could dominate their husbands, but they really preferred their previous size and just hoped their husbands had learned something from being in their shoes for the last few years. And yes, many women had learned things as well.

CHAPTER

20

A REAL FAMILY

While the Porters were enjoying dinner, Steve came up with a suggestion. "Wouldn't it be wonderful to continue the 'family' we have put together these past few years, even though things have returned to normal?"

"Yes," Bob said. "I don't want to lose contact with anyone, not after all you have done for me, the friendships we've built with people I'd never believed I could get along with."

"Well, why don't we invite everyone over again, and even include a few unsuspecting guests," Annie suggested.

"Like who?" Jane asked.

"How about Giovanni and his wife, Margaret?" Bob suggested.

"That's a good idea on the surface, Bob," Annie replied. "But they were Mafia thugs, and I don't think we would want them here."

"They're not Mafia thugs anymore. They've done a

great job turning that Italian restaurant their wives forced them to start into a really fine place to eat."

"Okay, yes, yes, let them come!"

The next "family" get-together was a spectacular potluck event with close to twenty people, including Giovanni and Margaret, now back to their original sizes, the same height, looking at each other eye-to-eye. Everyone hugged, and they laughed and cried all at once. They enjoyed wonderful salads, delicious chicken and incredible pasta furnished by the restaurant.

After the meal, the Porter and Carter teens trotted out their string instruments and performed some quartets. Giovanni, who had brought his violin, played some country music fiddle-style. He finished with a lively Vivaldi piece. Music. "Giovanni, how on earth did you learn country music as the head of, um, a traditional Italian family?"

"Well, it is Sicilian, not Italian. As a kid, I had to play a lot of Vivaldi, but I got hooked listening to country western when I first heard it on the radio. Something about it, I couldn't tell you what. At first I played it secretly, but then I just went back and forth between Vivaldi and country. Wanna hear what I did?"

He played for the next twenty minutes to an approving crowd, his style strong, quickly getting back in the flow, falling in love with his ability to play beautiful and fun music all over again.

It turned out to be a memorable evening. Near its

end, Bob stepped forward and said, "Well, everybody, we're a great gang here. We're all people who listened. It may have taken some jolts in our lives to wake us up, I know it did with me, but we have changed. Had the sphere not happened, I might still be bossing Jane around."

"Oh, Bob, it was so much fun to be two feet taller than you and push you around," Jane chuckled.

More laughter, more hugging and more promises for all to continue getting together every week and enjoy "family" togetherness, even though much of the work of MWT was already done. A renewed sense of harmony in society and households permeated the country.

"Before you all go, I want to say something," Annie said. Everyone stopped talking and turned. "I feel that eternal life and love are God's gifts to us all, and if we look up in our thoughts we will see the truth. For God is Love."

Still holding hands, the "family" softly added in unison, "And in this true eternal life we must love, love, love."

Guess what? The women's movements throughout the world continued to grow, record numbers of women were now in government offices and the women rising were embracing the world in their love.

The End

If you agree with our message, we would be so grateful if you were to pass on this book or suggest others to order it from online bookstores using my name as the author.

Any comments regarding "Women Rising" can be sent to the author at jsant@zirkel.us.

With my deepest gratitude I wish to thank Annie Garcelon, Anne French, Steamboat Writer's Group, Jan and Joe McDaniel, Nancy Harris, Elizabeth Carlson, Robert Yehling, Lisa Williams and my son-in-law, Gary Albright, for all the help they provided me to produce this book.

www.ingramcontent.com/pod-product-compliance
Lightning Source LLC
LaVergne TN
LVHW050927180725
816374LV00016B/132